Love

and

Infatuation:

THREE NOVELLAS

CHRISTOPHER ANDERSON

outskirts
press

LOVE AND INFATUATION

1.

An infatuation between Ann and me had reached a point at which I thought it not inappropriate to ask her out for drinks after work; what did I have to lose? It was Friday.

She paused and then agreed.

We met at a familiar pub close to work.

After two drinks each, I decided I shouldn't have another and then drive. I suggested we go to my place.

"Jeff." She gave me a sly look. "I'm married."

"Yes, I know. I'm not proposing marriage, only to come over for a cocktail."

She gazed into my eyes and didn't answer at first. I could see she was weighing the proposal. Her initial restraint furthered my attraction. It was obvious that she wanted to, and that encouraged me. But I didn't press the matter. She would say yes or no. She knew to what I was referring, and it certainly was not another cocktail.

She opened her eyes, and they widened in panic.

"Shit! What am I going to tell Derek!"

"Tell him you've fallen in love with a real man and are leaving him."

I was only half joking; I had already begun to fall in love, and now I had fallen the entire way. I admit: it's a fault.

"I'll think of something." She threw back the covers and dashed to the bathroom. A minute later, she was hurriedly gathering her clothes.

"Stay for coffee, at least."

"I can't."

"It will give you more time to think of an excuse."

She gave me an impatient look, as if the act of infidelity was entirely my fault.

"This was a mistake…a *huge* mistake."

"Don't say that." I was offended. I wanted to profess my everlasting love but knew that would only make her run faster and farther. I had been through this before.

I was forty years of age, never been married, no kids. I'd had my share of relationships, some serious, but nothing that had ever worked out. I wanted to be married, have kids, a house—the whole American Dream myth—but it had yet to happen. There was no reason for it not to happen, I didn't think. I was good-looking enough, I thought, kept in shape jogging at least three times a week, but the stars had yet to line up, bad luck, whatever—I didn't think that it was specifically anything about me that that put women off.

To make the matter worse, her husband was a doctor, and between the two of them, they made a substantial living. He had two children from a previous marriage.

But this infatuation, and consummation of it, was real. I carried a scintilla of hope.

2.

A nn avoided me at work. It broke my heart. Then one day, in fact exactly one week after she spent the night at my apartment, she walked into my office and sat down across from me.

"I can't stop thinking about what happened," she said.

"I can't either."

"And I can't stop thinking about you either."

"Either neither." My broken heart healed in an instant. "I feel the same."

"My husband's out of town."

I smiled.

"How 'bout I stop by your place after work for a cocktail?"

"Sounds wonderful."

With that she stood and left. However, she did not appear cheerful about our arranged rendezvous. She acted more as if we had just concluded some obligatory work transaction.

Was I in love? Was she? Gathering my senses, I realized love meant more than interest in a casual acquaintance and one night of sex. We were in the infatuation stage, which is more like the ingestion of an intoxicating drug than a rational state of stability. Having spent the past week in deep despair, like an addict going through withdrawal, I had now got my fix.

⸙

Ann arrived promptly after work. We got tipsy with several bourbons, then on to bed.

In the morning, I rose before her to fix coffee. She came into the kitchen with a smile, cheeks rosy, and sat down at the kitchen table. We talked about nothing much, mostly about work, and she never once mentioned her husband—which was fine with me.

"What do you want to do today?" I said.

"Do? I don't know… I had assumed I was going home."

"Let's make a day of it."

"And night?" She smiled.

It was the beginning of autumn, a chill in the air. The terrain was filled with reds and yellows of decaying leaves. We traversed downtown, to the Pike Street Market, then paraded onward to the Seattle Art Museum, where there was an impressionist exhibit: Monet, Manet, Matisse, Cezanne, Pissarro, Cassatt—it excited me to no end, sent me soaring along with my new love. I was mesmerized, staring at these original paintings

We had a late lunch at the Market Café, accompanied by cocktails, and then onward, to my home, and to bed. I couldn't believe my fortune.

———

In the morning, as we sat opposite each other at the kitchen table, I told her: "I'm crazy about you."

She didn't respond at first but then said, "You'll get over it."

"What? No. I won't. I've been in love with you from the start."

"You don't want to be in love with me, believe me."

"Why not?"

"You don't know me. If you did, you would not like it."

"I know you well enough to know that I love you."

I knew that it was stupidly premature to say that I loved her, and now of course I worried that she would end it.

She remained silent, a silence that told me she felt the same. How could she possibly not? How could this desperate love I felt for her not be reciprocal?

"I'm flattered, Jeff."

"But you don't feel the same."

"It's too early to mention love. Love is what I feel for my husband, and my parents and siblings. What you and I have is called 'infatuation.'"

How could she love him and be with me? I wanted to ask but didn't. I would bide my time until she eventually came around.

"My husband will be home tomorrow," she said, apparently signifying that we wouldn't be able to see each other for a while.

A few days passed in which nothing of relevance was said to each other, just business nonsense. Then, on Friday, she suggested we meet for drinks after work at our usual spot.

We sat at a booth with drinks, engaged in conversation, holding our hands across the table. I felt her love searing into me like electricity.

"Well, hello, you two lovebirds."

We looked up at Stan, a coworker. Ann sharply pulled back her hands.

"I thought there was something going on between you two." He nodded with a mischievous smile.

"There's nothing going on, Stan," Ann said.

"You don't have to worry; I won't say anything."

"A good friend of Jeff's has died. I'm consoling him."

I was startled by the blatant lie. I stifled a laugh.

"Uh-huh," Stan said. "Well, have a good weekend, you two." He winked, at me, laughed, and proceeded to the bar.

"It was stupid to meet here, so close to work."

I said nothing. It was stupid only if we cared that we were found out, which we were certain to be, after all.

"This is bad," she said. "I gotta go."

"You're not coming over?"

"Not now!" she said.

"What possible difference could it make now?"

She didn't answer. She stood abruptly, and I watched her scurry away. Stan watched her go and then turned to me with that obnoxious smile and tipped his drink. I ignored him. Smug asshole. I never had liked him. Whether or not he would tell the others, I had no idea, nor did I care, other than it might prompt Ann to end it.

But the very next day, in the late afternoon, after work, she texted and asked if I wanted to meet her at Ivar's for fish-and-chips.

Ecstatic, I walked from my apartment. It was about a mile, and walking was almost easier and sometimes even faster than driving these days due to the congestion and clogged streets.

It was a cold and blustery day. Thick, black clouds thrust in a southerly direction. I zipped my winter coat to my chin.

I was on time, and I got a text from her that she was just leaving her house. This annoyed me. I texted her back to meet me in the bar. After an IPA, my annoyance was replaced with cheerfulness when she arrived.

We retreated to a private booth. We ordered fish-and-chips and two IPAs. She attacked her food as if she hadn't eaten in a week. She ate anxiously, her cheeks and hands greasy, like a child's. She talked with her mouth full. I didn't listen to what she was saying, but she kept mentioning Derek. Derek this; Derek that.

"I think you've created this love for me out of thin air," she said.

She wiped her hands and face with a napkin and took a sip of beer, her intense ocean-blue eyes glowering into me uncomfortably through each gesture.

"*What!?*"

"Yes, I think it's true. You've created a fantasy."

"A fantasy?"

"Yes. Like some…novel or something." She shook her head, wiped her lips.

And with that, she finished off her food with a flourish. She sat back and sighed. She seemed content now, as if she had completed a task, as if we were at work. If that task was to hurt me, she had succeeded.

"That was good. I haven't had fish-and-chips in ages."

"Yes, it was tasty," I agreed, my meal only half-eaten.

Then she said, "I'm not leaving Derek, you know."

I didn't believe her. I believed she would eventually come around; I could not foresee any other possible outcome.

"It would be totally illogical for it to be otherwise," she said. "Even if I did love you—which I don't—from a financial viewpoint, it would make no sense."

"So, it's only the material stuff you care about."

"Not only, but it is a consideration. I would lose a small fortune. How much money do you have?"

"I have savings."

"Enough to put down on a house?"

"Not quite, but it's a goal."

"But as I said, I don't love you."

"Do you even like me?"

"Don't be ridiculous, of course I like you. I *love* fucking you."

"So that's it."

"Yes, I told you! I *said* you wouldn't like me if you knew me. I'm a bitch."

"No, you're not." I refused to believe that.

She sighed. "If I wasn't, I wouldn't be doing this."

That was it, I decided: she was feeling guilty. I actually liked that idea.

"Let's have one more beer," she suggested, "and I'll drive you home."

We had two more beers each; then we walked to her car and she drove me home.

At my apartment, she sat waiting for me to depart, engine idling.

"Aren't you coming in?"

"All right," she said, as if she had to wait for an invitation. She switched off the engine and unbuckled her seat belt.

We had an especially exuberant lovemaking session, as if relieving ourselves physically as well as psychologically, as if there was resolution of a dilemma. But there hadn't been, not as far as I was concerned.

We made love for over an hour. We each came twice.

I went into the kitchen and returned to bed with two IPAs.

"So what?" I said.

"What what?"

"Are we just going to be lovers?"

"What's wrong with that?"

"What if he finds out?"

"He'd better not!"

"I'll just be your boy toy."

"If you prefer to look at it that way. If it's more than that for you, then perhaps we should end it right now."

I decided to not believe her. I decided she was in denial of her love for me; she eventually would realize she loved me, leave her husband, and move in with me.

3.

"What we'll do is meet whenever feasible." She nodded as if thinking it through.

We had finished our meal and were going for a walk along the waterfront. The stroll wasn't as pleasing as it used to be here, now with the construction that was never-ending. It hurt the ears, the cars along Alaskan Way bumper-to-bumper, the sky ominous with cranes, vehicles navigating through one detour after another.

We were silent, and then suddenly, she stopped to hug me. If this wasn't love, what was? I decided she loved me but had yet to accept the fact.

"Leaving Derek isn't in the picture, you know," she said, as if sensing my thoughts.

I decided she had to say that for now. She was torn between her comfortable married life and the man she loved.

If I had believed otherwise, I would have ended it right then and there… No, sadly, that was not true…

She put her right arm into the crook of my left and squeezed. It felt right. I wanted to ask her wasn't she afraid someone we knew would see us but then thought it might mean she would let me go of my arm, and I certainly didn't want that. We continued to walk slowly and meditatively.

"Being with you is like being with a close friend," she said.

She kept doing that, alternating between lovingness and cruelty.

"Do you always walk arm in arm with friends?"

"Not always."

Jesus. More ambiguity. She was right: knowing her more meant I was beginning to hate her.

"I love having conversations with you," she went on, like that, like suddenly putting one piece of furniture here and then putting it back where it was before.

I thought this an odd statement, considering the lack of substance to our conversations, and we certainly weren't saying much now.

"Don't you have interesting conversations with Derek?"

"He and I have run out of things to talk about."

"But you still love him?"

"I suppose so."

I said nothing, but I was thinking that she no longer loved him, so it made sense to be in love with me.

"I loved touring that impressionist exhibit," she said. "You?"

There she goes again, I thought, *vacillating between affection and rejection.*

"Yes, of course."

"See? We have things in common."

"Do you read?"

"What a question. Of course I read."

"What are you reading now?"

"Right now, I'm reading *Where the Crawdads Sing.*"

"Haven't heard of it."

"It's been on the *New York Times* best seller list forever," she said, with a tone of snootiness.

I realized then why I hadn't heard of it.

"What do you read?" she said.

"Literature. I love Elena Ferrante, and I'm finishing up volume six of Karl Ove Knausgaard's *My Struggle.*"

"Haven't heard of either."

"We should go to the Elliott Bay Book Company sometime and browse."

"Is that a bookstore?"

"Yes."

"Where is it?"

"Uptown, Tenth and Pike."

She loved to read but had never heard of two of the current giants of literature and had never heard of the Elliott Bay Book Company, the iconic Seattle bookstore.

"Our sex is superb," she said, as if to make up for our lack of interest in particular kinds of writing. "But I love talking to you too."

4.

I was playing tennis with my usual partner and friend, Ken. Usually after one set, we rested and shot the shit, usually politics. Ken was a centrist Democrat while I was a Democratic Socialist, the result being naturally that our debates oftentimes became arguments. I couldn't seem to get past that huge knot in his head that there was little difference between moderate Democrats and Republicans, that they both pushed neoliberalism. I didn't think Ken even knew what neoliberalism meant. It occurred to me then I had no idea what political persuasion Ann was. I should ask but then thought maybe I would rather not know.

During this break, I told Ken about her.

"She's married?"

"Yes."

"Uh, fuck. Run for the hills, bro."

"I can't."

"You're whooped."

"'Fraid so."

"Does she feel the same about you?"

"I think so, but she's fighting it. She said she would never leave her husband."

"If you're going to keep seeing her, you'd better be able to accept that fact."

"She says that too, but I think she'll come around."

"Leave her husband and move in with you?"

14

"Yes."

"You are delusional, dude… I assume, asshole, the sex is great?"

"Oh yeah."

He laughed. "That would be enough for me. Come on, let's play. You were lucky last set."

The company needed a computer analyst. I was on the hiring committee, along with Ann and Jeremy, the HR director. After interviewing four applicants throughout the day, I mentioned one of them as the obvious choice; he was the most knowledgeable, was articulate, seemed reasonably intelligent, and presented himself well.

"No," Jeremy said, "he's no good."

"Why not?" I said.

"He wouldn't fit in."

"Fit in?" I was confused. I looked at Ann, and she shrugged. "Are you saying he wouldn't fit in because he's black?"

"That's not the reason, and you know it."

"Then what is it?"

"He just wouldn't fit here…our culture. I can just tell these kinds of things, Jeff. It's why I'm director of human resources."

I looked at Ann. "What do you think?"

She reflected, looking uncomfortable, and then said, "He aced the interview, Jeremy."

"All right!" Jeremy threw up his hands, obviously irritated. "Lord knows I don't want to be thought of as a racist! I'll bring him in for the second interview."

After work, at my apartment relaxing with a drink, I said to Ann, "I didn't know Jeremy was a racist."

"He's not a racist; he's just being practical."

"Then, you agree with him?"

"I agree that the applicant would be uncomfortable within our culture in the office. It has nothing to do with him being black."

"What culture! He's a computer analyst, not an alien from outer space! And even if he was, if he's right for the job, *fuck*!"

"Can we get off the topic?" she said, sighing irritably. "I came here to relax with a drink, not still be at work!"

At work Monday, the new computer analyst was there. And he was not the one I had recommended. Obviously, there had been no "second interview," at least not one where I had been included.

5.

Saturday morning, I left my apartment to go get something for breakfast. When I returned, I could see from a block away Ann at the entrance to my apartment, her phone at her ear. I reached for my phone and then realized that I had left it in the apartment. I tried calling out to her, but she couldn't hear me. I started running, but before I could catch her, she had got into her car and left.

I rushed inside and called her. When she didn't answer, I texted her. She didn't immediately text back. Shit. I began fixing breakfast. Then I received a text:

> I don't think you are aware of where we stand. I'll say it again: I don't love you. I love our time together, I love our sex, but I love my husband, and I will never jeopardize that. I do admire you. You're intelligent, well-read, and amazing at work. In fact, I believe you to be underappreciated. I'm also touched by your innocence, your puppy love for me. Maybe when we're old and fat, I will love you. who knows? Ann

The text annoyed me for the most part, but as usual, I saw some hopefulness in it, as well. She "admired" me. She found me intelligent, well-read, and good at my job. But the last part interested me most, the part about getting old together. She kept wavering between hope and futility with our relationship.

I texted: *Are you coming over?*
She texted back: *I might find some time tonight.*

We met at the Egyptian Theater, which was doing a retrospective of Ingmar Bergman. Ann had never seen a Bergman film, which surprised me at first and then not so much. Tonight, they were showing *Wild Strawberries*, a film that unlike most of his films was almost optimistic, with an uncharacteristic compassionate view of life.

In the theater, I felt Ann's warmth against me. She emanated a subconscious closeness, a mixture of eroticism and love. I held her hand in her lap, and it was comfortable; there was a smooth communication between us. Why couldn't she see this as love?

As we were leaving the theater, I asked her what she thought of the film.

"I'm not sure what it was about."

"Don't overintellectualize it. It's about an old man revisiting his past life and its regrets."

"We all have regrets in life. Unfortunately, we can't go back and change the past."

"And the film is as simple as that. I think it says that we should grab on to the present and make the most of things. That's what Sartre said, anyway."

"Who?"

"Jean-Paul Sartre."

"Oh."

But I didn't know if she knew who Sartre was. I wasn't sure if she had ever heard of existentialism, at least in terms of Sartre's philosophy, or even literally. I was almost afraid to ask.

We went to dinner at The Metropolitan. We had martinis with our steaks.

"For someone who's trying to save money for a place of your

own, you sure splurge on dining."

"Oh, I thought you were buying."

She looked at me as if I was serious. I wasn't, but I also saw no reason she couldn't pay for once.

I laughed, and she saw I was not serious.

"The gap I need for what I need to put down on a house and what I spend for a night out like this is the Grand Canyon, so huge it hardly makes much of a difference."

She stared at me, no doubt wondering how daunting it was for someone like me to get into a house or even a condo these days, perhaps thinking that it was impossible, which it virtually was.

At my apartment, I fixed more martinis, and then we made love. It was a near-perfect evening.

"Can you spend the night?"

"Yes, Derek is tending to his ailing mother for a few days."

We had satisfied ourselves sexually, and now she was going to spend the night to cuddle and sleep.

It was perfect.

6.

We spent more and more time together. Apparently, her mother-in-law was gravely ill, and Derek spent more time with her mother than with his wife. Fine with me. I hoped the old bat would linger for years.

Every Friday night after work, we went to one bar or another, and then back to my apartment for an athletic round of sex, a bite to eat, and sometimes she spent the night, sometimes not. I never begged her to stay; she would, or she wouldn't.

One night, we ran into an acquaintance of Ann's, and they chatted. He kept glancing at me, no doubt wondering why he wasn't being introduced, so I stepped forward.

"I'm Jeff."

He took my hand.

"Oh, I'm sorry," Ann said. "Jeff, this is Andrew. Jeff and I are coworkers."

"Ah," Andrew said, no doubt wondering why two coworkers would be out on a Saturday night.

As if to answer this thought, Ann said, "We had to do some OT in the office today to tidy up a few things."

"Ah," he repeated. "How is the old stomping ground?"

"Andrew used to work there," Ann explained, turning to me. "In fact, I believe you replaced him, Jeff," turning back to Andrew.

"Yes," Andrew said. "I miss it, but onward and upward, as they say."

I took this as an insult since it was obvious he was younger than I, a millennial for whom the sky was the limit.

"We were just going to get a bite," Ann said. "Why don't you join us?"

He paused as if to consider this but then politely declined.

At dinner, I reached across the table and joined my hands with hers.

"This is nice," she said.

"It is."

"Our relationship is nice. No complications with love, just enjoying our friendship."

"Friends don't have sex."

"Of course they do! We do, after all."

"But then…we're more than friends."

"Okay, lovers."

"Do you tell anyone about us?"

"No. Do you?"

"I told my tennis bud."

"Shit. Do you think that's wise?"

"He's not going to run off and tell your husband."

"Good," she said, as if I was serious.

"But people can figure things out on their own," I said.

"I would hate for that to happen."

"It probably already has. This evening, meeting Andrew, for example. You think he bought that crap about OT? We never work on weekends. And Stan, for another example."

"What about Stan?"

"He saw us that one evening."

"Oh, we explained that."

"You mean, we lied."

"Whatever. He can't assume things. We are just friends, after all. That's not a lie."

She kept going back to that, 'We're just friends', keeping her head in the sand.

"I'm married, after all."

"Yes, you're married. What we are having is called an 'affair.'"

"If you want to put it that way."

"It usually is put that way in everyday vernacular. How would you put it?"

"Friends with benefits."

I laughed, and then she did too, once realizing she had said a joke.

"Tell me," I said, "is that all this is?"

"What's that?"

"I'm just a friend you fuck."

"What's wrong with that?"

"Nothing, as far as it goes. But I want more than that."

"We've been through all this before. You're kicking a dead horse. If you want more, perhaps we should end it."

"I don't think you can."

"What?"

"No, I think you're in love with me, but don't want to admit it to me, perhaps even to yourself."

"That's absurd. It's just that I'm a monogamous person by nature."

"That just affirms my point."

"Okay, fine. We'll do it."

"Split up?"

"Not split up but see how long we can go without seeing each other."

"I don't want to do that."

"I don't either, but it will prove to you that I can do fine without you."

"But I can't live without you." I instantly hated myself for saying that.

"Okay," she said. "I'll not call or text. It will have to be you who resumes it."

"Our affair."

"Call it whatever you want, damn us to eternal hell!"

We laughed.

"To prove your point."

"Yes."

"And if I call tomorrow?"

She laughed, and then so did I. We really did have fun together.

7.

We were on our Christmas break from work. The company shut down from Christmas Eve till January 1. This was implemented more for practical reasons than generosity, since nothing much was accomplished during that period anyway. In exchange, they made us work some minor holidays, such as MLK Day, President's Day, and Go Milk Your Cow Day.

I assumed Ann would be busy with family stuff, so I didn't worry about contacting her. She apparently was serious about who would contact whom first, and so I waited to see what would happen. I got caught up on my reading and streamed several movies. It didn't stop me from thinking about her night and day. She was the first thought I had when I woke up in the morning and the last before I drifted off to sleep, my book in my lap, which I was unable to concentrate on anyhow.

Then I received a text:

How are you doing?

I smiled. She was the first to give in. Of course, she would probably deny that we had ever agreed to such a challenge to begin with. I now envisioned her going nuts not hearing or seeing me. I texted back:

I'm doing fine.

Are you dating anyone?

I chuckled. She was worried.

I wake up each morning with a different woman than the one from the morning before.

Ha ha. At any rate, you have that right.

This exchange renewed my confidence. It was only a matter of time before she accepted the love we had for each other and we would move in together.

8.

New Year's Eve I went to a party I had been invited to. I looked around and thought that I was the only person there unattached, and it made me sad. It made me angry with Ann all of a sudden. But then someone said hello. "It appears you and I are the only two here who are alone."

"We're not alone; there are all kinds of people here."

She laughed. "I mean, with a date."

"You're not with someone?"

She laughed again. What had I said that was funny?

"I'm Elena." She held out her right hand. I took it. She had a firm grip, as women seemed to have these days, asserting themselves.

"I'm Jeff."

"Who do you know here, Jeff?"

I looked around and started rattling off a few names, and then she interrupted:

"That's enough. Can I buy you a drink?"

"The drinks are free."

She laughed again. Again, I had said something stupid.

"Are you always this corny?"

"I'm afraid so."

She continued to laugh. "Come on."

She took my hand, and we meandered our way through the throng to the bar.

At the stroke of midnight, we were kissing. It was a meaningful kiss, and she followed me to my apartment in her car.

In the morning, she was gone. I thought this rude, but I didn't care so much. She meant little to me. But there was a note on the kitchen table. It read:

Had a good time.

Nothing else. No phone number. I thought: If I had done that to her, she would have been upset. Women are like men used to be. With Ann, I am the other man. She hadn't even sent me a happy New Year's text.

At work she seemed to be ignoring me. Then while I was in the lunchroom pouring a cup of coffee, she walked in.

"Hello, Jeff. How were your holidays?"

"Good."

I considered telling her about Elena to test her reaction but then thought better of it. It would have just made me look desperate and ridiculous.

"When are we getting together?" I said.

She looked around, even though she knew no one else was there.

She poured herself a cup of coffee and then looked up at me. "I'll talk to you later," she said.

What the hell did that mean? Did it mean she would talk to me later about getting together? Or did it mean she was going to talk to me later about ending it?

Two days later I sent her a text, again asking when we would be getting together, knowing how desperate this appeared, but I couldn't help myself.

Her answer arrived immediately: *"Friday night at The Comet."*

This was encouraging, because the Comet was close to my apartment, but discouraging at the same time, because why not just meet at my apartment?

Friday was cold, near freezing, ice-like clouds smothering the sky; jet-black when we got off work, stars invisible. I seldom went to the Comet despite its nearness to my apartment because it was a bit of a dive. The furniture was rickety and worn, and the walls hadn't been painted since god knew when and were scribbled with graffiti. But it had a reputation for being this way on purpose: a place where local artists, musicians, and writers hung out. Back in the late 1950s and early 1960s, the local Beats and folk singers such as Jim Page hung out there, and there was a framed photo on the wall of a disheveled and obviously drunk Jack Kerouac who had just come down from Desolation Peak in the Cascades where he had spent the summer as a fire lookout and from which would emerge his novels *Desolation Angels* and *The Dharma Bums.* In the late sixties and early seventies, it would naturally be hippies, and there was another photo on the wall of Jerry Garcia, and then yet another photo of Kurt Cobain.

In other words: not my thing.

"I love this place," Ann said, as soon as she had entered and sat down across from me at a booth.

"Really? Do you come here often?"

"Used to, before I was married."

"What do you want to drink?"

"I'll have what you're having."

I went to the bar to order two more IPAs. As usual, I was buying. The bartender looked like he was about eighty years old, though no doubt was twenty years younger, the raucous years etched into his face like a wrinkled and faded old map.

Ann and I talked about general things, work, the books we were reading, the films we each had streamed. The relevant topic stood beside us like a bright-pink elephant.

"Let's cut the bullshit, Elena."

"Elena?"

"I mean, Ann. Sorry."

"Who's Elena?"

"No one. A Freudian slip."

"A Freudian slip denotes that there is someone."

I looked at her and then confessed the one-night stand. My assertiveness as a man seemed to surprise her, even please her.

"Well!" she said.

"Aren't you angry?"

"Not at all. I'm happy for you. You're free as a bird, after all."

"Are you coming over?"

"Can't we relax a bit with a drink before rushing off to bed? Are you that fucking horny?"

"No. I'm sorry."

"Derek asked me over the holidays if I had a lover."

"Really? When?"

"Over the holidays, I said. He mentioned that I seemed anxious and depressed."

"Were you?"

"Yes, of course. I want you badly."

"Did you miss me?"

"Missed you, wanted you—same thing."

"What did you answer?"

"I said no, of course… We did make love once."

This meant they still had sex occasionally, and the thought disheartened me.

"We seldom make love anymore," she added, as if reading my mind.

Again, with that uncanny intuition of hers, she sensed that I didn't want to hear that. I wanted to hear that they never made love. This was absurd, of course; they were married, after all.

"Why do you think?"

"I don't enjoy sex with him anymore."

"What about him?"

"With him, he might as well be masturbating. Wham bam, turns over, and goes to sleep."

I laughed, and then so did she.

"It's actually not funny," she said.

"No, but I'm glad nevertheless."

"Why?"

"Because our sex is so spectacular."

"It is, isn't it? But you think if I left Derek and moved in with you, our sex wouldn't grow stale as well?"

"Never."

"You say that now. But the infidelity of it is what makes it exciting. The fact is, the human species was never meant to be monogamous. We've evolved with these silly moral constraints based on religion and economics."

"That's not universally true."

"You aren't the first, you know."

"What? First what?"

"Don't be obtuse—you know what."

"You've had other lovers?"

"Yes, of course."

I was shattered by this news. "Who was he?" I said, as if there had been only one, even though she said "others."

"It doesn't matter."

"Someone else at work?"

"Yes."

"How many times?" meaning how many times with one man, but I should have asked how many lovers.

"You remember Andrew?"

"That guy we ran into one night?"

"Yes."

"How many times?" I repeated.

"Not as many as you and me," she said, ambiguously.

I couldn't imagine there being someone else she had made love with more than she and I had, even her husband. Sick, I know. I persisted in thinking of myself as special.

"But he was married, and his wife was getting suspicious, so he broke it off."

"I think you hate yourself," I said, cruelly.

"I do. I don't like being unfaithful to my husband."

"Has he ever been to you?"

"I doubt it. He has a low sex drive."

There it was again, all about sex.

"Do you love him?"

"I don't think I'm capable of loving anyone. I don't even like dogs."

"You should tell Derek about me."

"Why should I do that?"

"To be honest with him."

"I don't want to make our marriage worse than it already is."

"Then you admit it's bad."

"I admit that all marriages have their ups and downs."

At the apartment, as I mounted her from behind, she said: "Harder."

I picked up the momentum.

"*Harder*, you *FUCK!*"

I slammed against her as hard as I could.

I came in buckets. We collapsed in a heap. I felt like a machine.

9.

Derek was spending long hours at the hospital, so she was able to come over to my apartment every night after work for a bout of lovemaking.

"This is getting out of hand," she said, one evening toward the end of January, lying in bed after making love.

"What is?"

"I'm becoming addicted to you…to the sex."

"What's wrong with that?"

"It'll mean you and I are in a permanent relationship."

"Aren't we?"

"I don't want to be. I just want us to be together occasionally. But each evening, I can't wait to get over here. My lust for you makes me woozy."

She reached into her purse and emerged with what looked like a vaping kit.

"What's that?"

"Pot."

"I didn't know you did that."

"Occasionally. It makes the sex better, not that it needs to be with us. Derek and I do it when we plan to have sex."

I didn't like knowing that.

She held it out to me, gesturing back and forth with her arm that I go first.

"I haven't smoked pot since college."

She made no comment on that, just kept signaling for me to take it.

I took a toke and immediately felt it hit my synapses. I was dizzy. The room spun.

I hardly remembered walking her out to her car. The harsh winter wind bit into me. I shivered uncontrollably.

Back inside, I pulled a blanket over me and sat mesmerized at what was on TV. I can't even remember what it was. CNN, I think. I hated CNN, same dull topics twenty-four hours a day.

I went to bed and tried to read. I couldn't concentrate. I couldn't sleep.

The next day I felt hungover. I decided I did not like marijuana.

Derek was going to be gone for the coming weekend, so Ann made a reservation for a cottage in Leavenworth, a touristy Bavarian-style village up off Highway 2 in the Cascades. It was a cold winter, so going up the pass, it was brisk and sunny, and the highway had been cleared of snow. Leavenworth was draped in white.

After checking in, we walked through town, window-shopping. We had lunch at The Watershed Café. Then we went for a short hike outside of town, then returned to our room and drank champagne in the hot tub, then got dressed and went into town for cocktails and dinner at the Andreas Keller restaurant.

When we returned to our room, we dived under the goose down blanket and into each other's arms.

In the morning, we went into town for espresso and breakfast.

Over breakfast, she stared out at the snow-covered mountains, said, "This is lovely, isn't it?"

"I love you," I said.

She continued to stare dreamily at the crisp outside and didn't respond.

After breakfast, we went for another vigorous hike and then

returned to our room and had coffee and Kahlua in front of the fire.

We made love each morning and night. There was no hurry as there usually was at my apartment, where she was usually rushed.

I of course loved this, and her. How could she not reciprocate? She remained imprisoned within a shroud of denial. I, for one, could not make love to a woman I did not love. I had never been able to, never been to a prostitute, even during periods of celibacy. I could not be with a woman who did not reciprocate desire and feelings for the other person, with someone who was there solely for money. I thought it humiliating and degrading, for both parties. I knew some men liked that power they had over helpless women in such situations, the women subservient to their capital. I found it depraved, though I was empathetic of some women forced into that life.

"I'm glad you made this reservation," I said.

"What? You made it."

Why did she say that?

"It was a consensus," she said.

"All right. If you say so."

In the morning on another hike before breakfast, it was snowing. The flakes were like white, corrugated, fifty-cent pieces dancing in the air. We kicked through the growing pile on the trail, the tall pines and Douglas fir being clothed with snow. We felt the silence, smelled the verdant forest.

Over breakfast, her phone rang. She looked at it but didn't answer. She sent a text.

"Derek?" I said, and she nodded.

"Nothing could be better than this, having breakfast by the fire, looking out at the snow-covered mountains, making love to the person you love."

"Let's hurry back to the room."

Making love, I on top of her, she stared above my head at the ceiling and grunted with each thrust. She came, and then I did.

Resting on top of her, she said, "You're the only person who's been able to do that."

I pushed up and said, "Do what?"

"Make me come during intercourse."

"Really?" I was pleased.

"Yes." She shrugged. "It's always before required either digital or oral…It's one reason why Derek and I seldom make love anymore. It takes work, and he can't be bothered."

"Why do you think I do that to you?"

"Because you're intense. You're determined to please me. And you're…"

"What?"

"You're big."

I laughed. "We belong together."

"We are together," she said, rhetorically.

"I mean, permanently."

"Nothing is permanent, Jeff. This won't be either. Tomorrow we'll be back at our desks, and this will recede into nothingness. Let's just enjoy it while it's here."

As we drove back to town, her left hand remained resting on my right thigh. As we swerved down Highway 2, the forest was still and the trees were crowned with frozen white. Not a word was spoken. I didn't know what to make of it, whether to be comforted or worried.

Then she said: "This is wrong. I'm not being fair to you."

"How so?"

"I'm talking advantage of you. I'm just with you for the sex."

"That's not true. You love me."

"I love our sex."

"You love me but don't want to."

I dropped her off at her car, which was parked in my parking space at the apartment.

"See you tomorrow," she said, dryly.

But then she walked around the front of my car and came to my window. I lowered it, and she kissed me shortly on the lips. "Love you," she said.

"I love you too." I watched until she was seated in her car and started it up. She looked at me, smiled and waved, and then she drove out of the lot.

She said she loved me.

10.

I didn't expect to hear from her, but later, while I watched TV, she called:

"Whatcha doin'?"

"Watching an old movie on TV."

"Which one?"

"*The Choice*, with Douglas Fairbanks Jr."

I doubted that she had heard of it. I doubted that she knew who Douglas Fairbanks was, junior or senior.

"Do you want to keep watching?"

"I've put it on pause."

I turned off the sound.

"I had a good weekend," she said.

"It was wonderful, Ann."

The line was silent for a moment.

"Did you mean what you said?" I said.

"What did I say?"

"You said you loved me."

"It's just an endearment."

I was about to say, "Bullshit," but held my tongue.

———✣———

We didn't talk to each other at work about anything relevant to our relationship all week, and I became depressed, thinking that she didn't mean it when she said she loved me. I was beginning to weary of this charade.

Saturday I was walking along Fifteenth Avenue to have lunch at the Coastal Kitchen when I saw Ann approaching accompanied by a middle-aged man whom I assumed to be Derek. I didn't see anything special about him, average height, average looks, a bit heavy around the middle.

"Hello, Jeff," she said, as casually as if it were just another day at the office.

"Hi!"

"Derek, this is Jeff. We work together."

And fuck, I thought, as I took his hand. He shook my hand sincerely with a firm grip and smiled. I saw nothing suspicious in his look. He made no mention of ever hearing of me.

"What are you doing here?" I said, since it was nowhere near where they lived.

Her face turned pale, and I realized I shouldn't have said that.

"We're just in town for the day," she said.

"We're looking to get some lunch right now," Derek said. "Would you like to join us?"

I wanted to say yes, but I could tell by Ann's expression that I shouldn't.

"I've eaten," I lied. "But thanks."

"Nice meeting you," he said, shaking my hand again, just as sincerely as before.

"You as well." And we departed on our separate ways.

A few steps away, I turned back to them, and she seemed to sense that and turned to look at me over her shoulder. Derek didn't seem to notice. There seemed nothing in him that suspected a thing.

Just then my phone rang. I looked at it and was surprised to see the name Erin Jorgensen pop up. I didn't answer.

Erin was an old girlfriend. We'd once had an intense relationship, torrid and tumultuous. She was always breaking up with me and then summoning me back, keeping me in a constant schizophrenic state of euphoria and then suicidal depression. I finally tore myself away for good, refusing to see her anymore. I'd heard since she'd gotten married.

I listened to her voice mail: "Hello, stranger. Just thought I'd check and see if you were still alive."

I called her back when I got home.

She answered. "Hello, Jeff!"

"How are you, Erin?"

"I'm fine… Actually, I'm not fine. My husband and I are separated and going to get a divorce."

"Sorry to hear that."

"Don't be. It's for the best. He's a cheater."

I thought that ironic coming from her. I'd heard that they'd had money and had bought a house on the east side overlooking Lake Washington.

I said nothing to that. I was still bitter about what she had done to me.

"Would you like to get some dinner?" I said.

"That would be nice. We'll catch up."

Over dinner, she related to me the disaster that was her marriage, a two-year nightmare.

"Did you have kids?"

"No, thank goodness."

I sipped my martini.

"It didn't take me long to realize I never should have broken up with you."

"Things happen for a reason."

"You really believe that?"

"No."

We laughed.

After three martinis, I told her about Ann.

"Sounds like you and me."

"Not exactly."

"No, of course not."

After we'd finished our meal, she said: "Would you like me to come over?"

"For old time's sake?"

"Yes. Why not?"

"You hurt me badly, Erin."

"You were the one who broke up with me, if you remember."

"We were always fighting. You were always running off with someone else."

"True."

We laughed. "I'm going to decline your offer for now."

"A rain check?"

"Yes, maybe later." But I had no intention of reopening that wound.

"You certainly have no obligations to a married woman!"

"You're married, you said."

"But we're getting divorced."

We'd had too many cocktails, and after too many more, I changed my mind, and she followed me to my apartment in her car.

In the morning over coffee, she said to me: "I don't know what this means, Jeff."

"You always say that."

"I do?"

"Yes. After reuniting after a breakup, you would always say 'I don't know what this means, Jeff.'"

"Well...what did it mean?"

"It meant we were back together. For now."

"And what does it mean this time?"

"This time it doesn't mean a thing, Erin. I'm over you finally."

She stared at me knowingly. She could see that it was true.

Later I decided to go for a run and then catch the Seahawks game.

During the game, Ann called.

"You're too much of a romantic," she said first thing when I answered.

"Where'd that come from?"

"You take our relationship too seriously."

"I love you. I can't help that."

"Love should include the intellectual."

"Your point?"

"We don't have that much in common intellectually."

"I don't think that is mandatory."

"No, not at the beginning, during the infatuation stage. But if it is to last, a couple should have more things in common than we do."

I thought about this and couldn't think of what to say.

"What if I told you I voted for Trump?"

I paused to consider this impossible horror. "But you didn't... did you?"

"No, of course not. But I did vote for Hillary."

"Most people did. It's not a deal breaker."

It was obvious the Seahawks were going to lose, so I turned off the TV. "Love just happens to people, something beyond rhyme or reason. You know the old saying, 'Love is blind.'"

"I'm resisting it."

"I know you are."

My spirits lifted. She loved me too but was fighting it. It made perfect sense, after all. She didn't want her marriage uprooted.

"I can come over if you like."

"Where's Derek?"

"Playing golf. He'll be gone for hours."

I looked outside as if to doubt what she said about golf on a winter's day and saw that it was indeed sunny.

"It will be dark soon."

"He always goes into the clubhouse for drinks afterward."

"He belongs to a private club?"

"Do you want me to come over or not?"

"Come on over."

She arrived promptly, and we hurried to bed. Then, after making love, she just as hurriedly started dressing.

"Fuck and go?"

"I do need to get home before Derek."

"Was it worth it?"

"The sex? Of course. I love fucking you."

"All right. Hurry home to Papa."

"Fuck you."

I hadn't meant it as a joke, but we laughed, nevertheless.

"I'd like to spend more time with you than just a quick fuck."

"You're making me feel bad about coming over at all."

"No, it was good."

She pecked me on the lips and turned to leave.

"I love you," I called out before she shut the door.

She didn't respond.

11.

There was a rainstorm that lasted for days. It was torrential, like nothing I had ever seen before in the Northwest. Rain was bucketing down streets like rivers and cascading down stairs like waterfalls. It was bizarre, nearly biblical. Fortunately, Seattle is hilly, and the rain just flowed into Puget Sound. However, up in the mountains, where it was supposed to be snowing this time of year, rivers were overflowing and flooding homes at the foothills and valleys.

I was looking outside my window, on the phone with Ann. "I thought we were going to see each other today."

"I'm not going out in this torrent!"

"Oh. Okay."

She seemed to sense my disappointment and said: "Don't make me feel guilty."

I said nothing to that, but I wanted to say: *So, I'm not supposed to guilt-trip you, but you are free to disappoint me whenever you feel like it.*

"Maybe if it lets up later," she then said.

"Okay, but it's not showing any signs of doing that."

"No."

"It's all right. I hate not seeing you of course, but I'll just stay busy cleaning or reading. I have some reading I need to catch up on anyway."

There was a pause, and then she said: "You know, actually, I could call an Uber; then I wouldn't have to search for a parking

44

space by your apartment."

"That's an idea."

That was what she did. An hour and a half later, she was downstairs ringing my bell. I was surprised she had arrived so quickly. I rang her in, and she rushed in drenched from just running from the Uber car to my front door.

I handed her a towel, and she scrubbed her head. She was one of these fortunate women who didn't have to worry over her hair; she was able to just let it fall where it lay, and it still looked great.

I poured two bourbons, and we sat.

"I hate you for making me come out in this storm."

"I didn't make you."

"You made me feel guilty, so I had to come." She kept scrubbing at her scalp.

I was tired of defending myself, so I said nothing.

"It is quite a storm, isn't it?"

"Are you being rhetorical?"

We laughed.

We sipped our drinks and looked out at the storm. It was very calming from this viewpoint, inside warm and dry.

"I suppose global warming has something to do with it," she said in a resigned way, as if exhausted by the topic.

We finished our drink, and we went to my bedroom to undress.

"Do you want to butt fuck me?" she said.

"What! Where'd that come from?"

"Most men do at some point."

"Do you want me to?"

"No, it hurts."

"Then why did you ask?"

"To get the subject out of the way."

"Well, then, to answer your question: no, I have no interest in inserting my penis into the orifice of which the purpose is specifically for excreting fecal waste."

She laughed. "Mouths are for eating, breathing, and drinking, but you like it when I blow you."

"Mouths and tongues have multiple purposes."

We laughed.

"So…I assume you've done that," I said.

"Anal sex? Yes, but like I said, it hurts. Women who succumb to that do it for the man, not themselves."

"With your husband."

"No, not with him."

I was about to ask with whom, but in fact, I really didn't want to know.

We lay naked under the covers.

"You don't seem to have any friends."

"There's Ken," I argued.

"Who's Ken?"

"Someone I play tennis with."

"So, you socialize with him?"

"Not much."

"See? You have no friends. I think that bothers me."

"Why?"

"It makes you more dependent on me."

"You have lots of friends, I suppose."

"Not lots, but yes. It's not normal not to have friends. It makes you reclusive…or something."

"I've had friends, in school and so forth, but people move on with their lives. Out of sight, out of mind. I'm not the kind who's sentimental about friends. And it's hard for me to find people I have things in common with… To tell you the truth, I don't like people very much. I hate Facebook and Twitter."

"What! You don't like people?"

"I find most people rather inane."

"You and I don't have much in common, but we're friends… aren't we?"

"You and I are lovers."

"Mostly friends."

"First it's anal sex; now it's friends. What's going on, Ann?"

"We don't always have to have sex, do we?"

"No, of course not."

"I come over, and we fuck—that's it."

"What do you want to do, then?"

"Why don't you go get more whiskey?"

I got up and went to get the bottle and two glasses.

We lay in bed naked with the blankets pulled over us, sipping our whiskey and watching the rain.

"This is nice," she said.

"Yes, it is," I agreed. I sipped and stared outside, the storm pummeling the window.

"We don't always have to fuck, you know."

"I know."

"You all right with that?"

"Of course. I love making love to you, but if you're not in the mood, that's all right too. I'm fine with sipping bourbon and watching the rain."

"Me too." She smiled. "Tell me about your past girlfriends."

"Not much to tell."

"Oh, come on. Start from the beginning. Did you have a girlfriend in high school?"

"For one school year, my senior year. Then we went to separate colleges, and that was that. We kept in touch for a while, but then she said she was with someone else."

"Did you have sex with her?"

"Clintonesque sex."

She laughed. "So, she blew you."

"Yes."

"It's curious how some young women think, that sucking cock is not sex just because there is no penetration."

"I know, right? Since there is—in the mouth."

We laughed.

"Well, it was high school," I said. "Did you have sex in high school?"

"We were talking about your girlfriends."

"All right." In truth, I didn't want to know if she did. "I was in a relationship in college for two years, until I discovered that she was screwing my roommate."

"How did you find out?"

"He told me."

"Why did he do that?"

"Because he didn't care about her in a romantic way, the way I did. He was my friend. I suppose he felt he was being loyal to me."

"Curious sense of loyalty."

I laughed. "Yes. Of course, it ruined the relationship I had with both of them."

"Something tells me you've had poor luck in relationships."

"You think?"

We laughed.

"Go on," she said.

I told her about Erin, since in a sense she encapsulated all my relationships into one, perhaps my most serious relationship.

"She was always breaking up with me, usually when she met some guy who interested her. She called herself a Christian and felt she was not cheating on me if she broke up with me so she could go fuck some guy and then summon me back when she was done with him."

"If she called herself a Christian, then technically, wasn't she?"

"I guess in her mind. She was one of those Christians who

believed it was okay to go to war with other countries and kill people for no reason. She supported Bush's war in Iraq."

"I'm surprised you would be with a woman like that."

"No shit. She probably voted for Trump. I had fallen before I discovered it, when it was too late... Anyway, on one of these break-ups, she found someone more suitable for her and married him."

"And you haven't talked to her since?"

"No," I lied. I didn't tell her the rest. I didn't like lying, but I thought it best this time, a white lie, as it were.

"So? Go on?"

"That's about it, my relationships in a nutshell."

This wasn't quite true, but I was tired of the topic. I didn't tell her that I was nearly always in a relationship, always searching for "the one." I didn't want to know about Ann's love life. I wanted her to be "the one," the Madonna. But she wasn't. In the classic Madonna/whore dichotomy, she was more the latter.

12.

We were out to dinner. We had drunk a bottle of red wine were and working on the second. We were at Salty's in West Seattle, on Harbor Avenue, gazing across Elliott Bay at the downtown buildings, tall, sparkling bright reflections against the sun.

"I don't know what I want," Ann said out of nowhere, speaking what was on her mind.

"Right this moment, you obviously want to be with me."

"Obviously." We laughed.

She caught the waiter's eye and raised the empty bottle, gesturing for another.

"If I left him now, it would be total chaos. I'm too old to start over."

The waiter arrived, popped the cork, and refilled our glasses.

"You know what you want," I said, "but you're afraid to embark on it."

"I'm not sure that's true. I'm a difficult person to love, Jeff."

"Not to me; you're easy."

She laughed. She drank down half the glass.

"And I worry about Derek."

"Of course you do, because you're not the monster you think you are."

"If it weren't for that, it would be easy."

"Yes, of course."

"We'll just have to carry on as it is and see how things turn out."

I decided she was willing to leave him but just not ready. This was easy to understand, after all. No one likes change; I knew that as much as anyone. I was a conformist. I liked things to move along smoothly without having to think about it too much. But one had to submit to change, especially these days. If you didn't keep up, you were left behind. Right at my heels were the millennials with more high-tech skills than I had, and right behind them was Generation Z, with even more skills. And behind them were babies in the womb having already evolved to face the challenges of ever increasingly rapid changes. I read that somewhere.

"I wish you could spend the night with me."

"I wish I could too."

Outside, it was cold, near freezing. We stood just outside the door and kissed goodbye before separating to our respective vehicles.

"I love you," I said.

She didn't return the sentiment.

Back at my apartment, I poured a glass of bourbon. Having driven home legally drunk, I wanted to be really drunk. I contemplated the situation in silence, sipping my whiskey and enjoying the taste and the way it soothed my throat. In some ways, I was encouraged. She still wouldn't say she loved me, but I knew she did. She was being cruel, cruel to her husband, cruel to me. It was simple: we needed to be together for the rest of our lives. But she was making that complicated.

Once again, I had fallen in love with someone who was not good for me. She was evil.

My phone rang. It was Erin.

"I'm in the neighborhood."

13.

Spring arrived. The air was alive with blossoms and optimism. Ann and I were able to get together once in March and once in April. Each time she mentioned Derek as an impediment to seeing each other more. I felt she was delaying the inevitable, putting me off. In these same two months, Erin had come over four times. I didn't love Erin anymore, thank god, but I was using her as a sort of leverage, and sort of an act of revenge, even though Ann didn't know about her.

"Seems like you got the right kind of problems to me," Ken said, between sets one day.

"What do you mean?"

"You have two women. Boohoo."

"But you have Tina."

"Yes, of course, and I love her. But sex with one woman gets old after a while. I would cheat on her if I could get away with it."

"Why don't you discuss it with her?"

"Are you kidding? Discuss what?"

"Maybe you can come to some sort of arrangement."

"An open marriage? She would never agree to that!"

"You never know. You might be surprised."

"No way! I don't want my wife fucking other men."

"But you want to fuck other women."

"It's different with men."

I laughed. "Oh, right. Come on, man, it's not the Middle Ages

52

anymore—there are no more chastity belts."

"Fuck you. Let's play."

One evening Ann arrived with a flower arrangement. I was pleasantly surprised by the gesture. However, I think it was more for herself than for me, as she went about arranging it, trimming the ends, putting it in a vase, adding water, and placing it carefully on the desk at my front window.

I poured two bourbons, but before they were drunk, we were frantically making love. I was behind her at this same front window, her arms balanced on the desk, her face erotically tickling the flower arrangement with each thrust. I fantasized people walking by and seeing us, even though that was impossible, unless they walked on air.

Afterward, she devolved into the same old argument that I didn't understand that what we had wasn't a romantic relationship but a sexual one. "We're fuck buddies," she said.

"Then why don't you leave?"

"What? Why?"

"We fucked, so why don't you leave?"

"Can I finish my drink first? Jesuschrist, you're sensitive!"

"It's exhausting for me, you being so flippant about our relationship. What if I told you I was seeing another woman?"

"Are you?"

"Why not? You're married; I'm free as a bird."

"Yes, you are, but no, you wouldn't do that. Not if you are as serious about me as you say you are."

There she went again, turning everything back and forth, up down, inside out, topsy-turvy. I'd about had it.

She took my right hand into hers and squeezed. Her hand was warm, mine cold. We sat there silently.

I poured more bourbon. I put a record on the stereo, *John Wesley Harding.*

"You love this old shit, don't you?"

"Dylan has no time limitations. He's immortal."

She shrugged.

Who didn't adore Bob Dylan?

As we hugged goodbye, I could feel the tension between us. I wanted to say I loved her but didn't for once. I decided, from then on, I would wait for her to say it first.

Later I texted her and said maybe it would be better if we not see each other until we could come to a decision about our relationship.

What decision? she texted back.

I didn't respond. I was exhausted. I poured another drink and picked up the novel I was reading, *Flight,* by Olga Tokarczuk. It was the most brilliant prose I'd read since Knausgaard. The current literary giants of the world were not American: Elena Ferrante, Milan Kundera…Tokarczuk had just been selected for the 2018 Nobel Prize in Literature, belatedly.

14.

Two months passed, and Ann and I didn't see each other besides at work. During these two months, Erin came over twice. We really were fuck buddies.

"Are you seeing anyone else?" she asked one of these nights.

"No," I said, which seemed literally true at the moment.

I said nothing else, and she said:

"Aren't you going to ask if I am?"

"No."

She stared at me meditatively for a moment and said, "I should probably make you wear a condom."

"If that's so, then you needn't come over anymore. Wearing condoms is like fucking air."

"I know. I hate them too… I'm not seeing anyone else, by the way."

I shrugged indifferently. I knew that this could be true or not, knowing Erin. I really didn't care either way. It occurred to me that I was treating Erin similar to how Ann treated me, other than I continued to hold on to the fantasy that Ann really loved me.

"I don't think I should come over here anymore."

"Suit yourself," I said, cruelly.

"You're an asshole."

I looked at her. "I'm sorry Erin. I don't mean to be."

She smiled, as if I really did not mean to be. "Okay."

One Friday there was a retirement party at work. Eugene was sixty, and he didn't really want to retire. Or, that is, he couldn't afford to retire, but realized he had outgrown his usefulness at work. That's what he told me at the party: "outgrown," as if he had evolved beyond the confines of this work environment. The truth was that technology had outgrown his usefulness. He couldn't keep up and so had given up. He couldn't collect Social Security for two more years and had no pension other than the piddling 401K that they provided there at that cheap-ass place, 3 percent or some worthless number close to it.

"So, stay," I said, shrugging. "Sit at your desk and do nothing. You wouldn't be the only one here doing that."

"They pressured me. I was told to retire or be let go. Fortunately, our mortgage is paid off, and my wife is still working, though she will want to quit too at some point. She's my age."

"Can you collect unemployment?"

"I haven't thought of that. I've never done that."

"It's no disgrace. Talk to Jeremy and see if they can say you're laid off rather than retiring."

"Ah." He nodded with insight.

"You'll have to keep pretending to look for work, though, in order to qualify."

"That won't do, then. I could end up being a greeter at Walmart or something."

"The way I understand it, you don't have to accept anything outside your job skills or less than your current salary."

"Really?"

"You'll be fine," I said but then, sadly, really did picture him as a greeter at Walmart.

Later, I saw him talking to Jeremy, who seemed to be nodding back at him reassuringly.

Derek was there with Ann. It was apparent he knew Eugene, as he shook his hand and congratulated him. It was incongruous: Derek was rich; Eugene was poor.

Derek went around the room and introduced himself to the others like a politician.

While he was thus engaged, I went over to Ann. She smiled, but I knew it was fake.

"I miss you," I said.

"I'm surprised, after the way you talked to me last time we were together."

"I was just exasperated."

"You said maybe we shouldn't see each other anymore."

"I didn't mean it."

She said nothing to that.

"I'm worried about Eugene," I said.

"Why?"

"He can't afford to retire."

"No?"

It surprised me, her lack of empathy about that which to me was obvious. She was insulated within her world of comfort. She didn't want to lose that, and I could hardly blame her. She was probably worried that I would be another Eugene. And I have to admit, I was worried myself. We all were, these days. We couldn't keep up with the demands of capitalism. But it would soon be over anyway, I thought to myself fatally, thinking of drowning polar bears.

"Do you ever think you could have lived your life differently?"

"Do you?"

I sighed with frustration at her typical nonanswer. "I think we're all products of circumstance. Eugene could have been a longshoreman and retired years ago with a fat pension. But he chose to be an office worker, and technology soared past him."

"Aren't you the philosophical one today."

I was about to say, "It's capitalism," but knew it would only irritate her. Capitalism had been good to her.

"You have nothing to worry about," she said.

"What do you mean?"

"You're too smart. You'll always be useful here."

"You mean they won't be pushing me out the door at sixty?"

She looked at me. She seemed about to say something but didn't.

"Why do you continue working?" I asked. "You don't need to."

"How do you know?"

"Oh, come on! Derek's a doctor—that's how I know."

"You think we're rich?"

"I think you're definitely in the top 1 percent."

She scoffed. "We're middle-class. Most of our acquaintances are much better off than we are."

"What does he make?"

"None of your business."

"Well, I know it has to be in the six figures."

"Yes. So?"

"So, what? Three, four hundred?"

"The truth is, I don't know."

And there it was, her damned ambiguity. She didn't know the exact figure of her husband's salary. I didn't know whether or not she needed to continue working.

"When are we going to get together?"

"I *am* desperately horny for you."

"There's that at least."

"We'll see."

"See what? I know you love me. Is that it?"

"Don't go there." She was trying hard to restrain her irritation. "Not here. We'll talk later. I'll text you."

And she was off to congratulate Eugene.

15.

There was the husband, and there was the lover. That was the bottom line, the reality I could not seem to accept. I could not seem to abandon the fantasy of us eventually getting married. I thought about telling her that I still saw Erin, to see if she would be jealous, but I was terrified that she would react with rage and end it. She wouldn't understand that I would happily give Erin up if she would agree to marry me.

I couldn't bear the idea that I was no more than "the lover." If I were a woman, I would be the "mistress." I was nothing more than a tool to satisfy her physical lust. My penis was a warm vibrator.

She compartmentalized our life as one entity separate from another. I was a category in her file documents that interplayed between one reality and the other. I existed as a plaything, my presence in her life no different than Ken's in mine, when I satisfied my physical needs on the tennis court.

But even on the tennis court, it was more than physical; it was emotional as well, the satisfaction of winning opposed to the emotional pain of losing.

In a twisted way, she was faithful to her husband. For all I knew, Derek had a lover too. Perhaps they had an understanding. I thought I must ask her. So, I did:

"Does Derek have a lover?"

"No, of course not. Don't be ridiculous."

She had managed to come over. We were sitting up in bed with our drinks after making love, my favorite time of us being together.

"The idea is not ridiculous at all. You have a lover; it only makes sense that he has one."

"He's too busy for a lover. That's why I'm here; he got called away on an emergency. And I told you: he has a low sex drive."

I found this naïve. "How do you know for sure? Maybe he has a low sex drive only with you. Maybe he was called away by his mistress."

She looked at me as if wondering that this possibility could be true. "No," she said, as if to reassure herself.

"He's probably just as confident of your fidelity as you are of his."

"I would never tolerate that."

I laughed. "That's a bit hypocritical, don't you think?"

"If you insist on continuing with this nonsense, I'm going to leave. I should probably leave anyway."

"All right."

She looked at me. "I'm with you now because I can't stay away. I don't feel good about it. I'm ashamed of myself."

"You love me."

"Perhaps a little." She smiled teasingly.

"Why else can't you stay away?"

"You know why," she said, from which I inferred it was the sex. "Anyway, even if I do love you—which I don't—I will never leave Derek. You need to accept that fact. At some point, this must end."

"When you get tired of me."

"Maybe."

And with that, she got out of bed, dressed, and kissed me goodbye.

She wanted me to believe she couldn't stay away because of the sex and that she loathed herself because of it. The lover was separate from the person. And it was true that we away from each other were separate beings. We didn't even have a lot in common; she had pointed that out. It was as if I was a gigolo, and the fact that I entertained two lovers who seemed to come to me solely for sex denoted that.

And yet (I argued with myself), it was only Erin who came to me specifically for sex. Ann and I did things outside the bedroom: we went out to eat; we went for walks along the waterfront; we vacationed in the snowy mountains; we went to movies. We enjoyed our time together outside of the bedroom; she had even said so.

It gave me hope. But then the opposing argument surfaced in my mind: I was number two in her life; Derek was number one, and this thought would push me into depression again. I was being driven mad.

16.

She managed to find a way for us to get away to their vacation property at Lake Chelan. She picked me up in her 2019 Land Rover Discovery. They had a beautiful home posted on the hill two miles north of town on the east side of the lake, which offered a beautiful view of the lake and the surrounding hillsides. It was late spring, and her property was bursting with colors. On the north and south sides of the house were tall pines, which shaded the house in summer and insulated it in winter, while still allowing the sun to penetrate the passive solar heat through the tall western-faced windows. They had a wood-burning stove, which she immediately began to prepare as soon as we arrived, since it was cold.

Lake Chelan was more a fjord than a lake, formed after the last ice age. It was fifty miles long and at its south end emptied into the Columbia River. At the northernmost tip was the town of Stehekin, accessible only by boat, where the inhabitants lived a Spartan life with no electricity. The water was untainted because there were no factories polluting the lake. Water from their faucets came straight from the lake and was ice cold.

She was telling me all this as we had dinner at a restaurant in Wapato Point, farther north on the east side of the lake close to the town of Manson. We sipped our cocktails and looked out at the lake as it wound north between the pine-dense hillsides.

I had never been here before but had always wanted to. We had the entire weekend to ourselves, having driven straight here after work. We would stay Saturday and then return to Seattle Sunday evening.

"Why don't we call in sick Monday morning and stay another day?" I suggested, half-seriously.

"All right," she said, which surprised me, since obviously it would look suspicious, us both being gone at the same time. And there was the husband.

"No, we'd better not," she said, having thought it over. "I wish we could."

It was these times together when my heart soared with optimism for our future life together. I sipped my drink and fantasized Ann divorcing her husband and us moving here. He would get the house in Seattle, and she would get the Chelan house. We would quit our jobs and pool our resources.

"What's great about Chelan," she went on, "is that during the hot summer there is a comforting breeze that wafts through the valley, while in the winter, the air is still and you can sit out on the lawn chairs with your down coat on and soak in the sun."

"You," she had said. "Your." Me. Mine. I knew she was just being dialectal, but I took it that way, carrying on with the fantasy.

"Sounds like Camelot," I said.

"Camelot? Why?"

"Haven't you seen the musical?"

"No."

I didn't bother to explain. "We'll see it sometime. We'll stream the movie with Richard Harris and Vanessa Redgrave."

"Who?"

I looked at her in disbelief. Did I even know her?

Saturday morning, we sat out on "our" sun-bleached lawn chairs with our coffee and drew in the sun. Then we had breakfast at

Campbell's Inn staring up the lake.

"Look," I said.

An eagle was circling the lake not far from the restaurant.

"I'm glad we came," she said, smiling at me.

"I am too."

"It's funny how you say it that way."

"Funny? Why's that."

"'I am too,' rather than 'Me too.'"

"It's the grammatically correct way to say it," I said, as if she didn't understand that.

"Yeah, but somehow it sounds condescending."

"'Condescending'? What does that mean?"

I laughed, and then she did.

In the evening we had cocktails on her deck and watched the sun set beyond the mountains, the lake sparkling gold. Then she fixed a tuna casserole for dinner with white wine and a chocolate cake we had picked up at a bakery in town. It was all delicious and domestic. We made love on a blanket in front of the wood-burning stove.

In the morning we had coffee and muffins at this same bakery and then decided to take the long way home on the North Cascades highway, up the Methow Valley alongside the Methow River, past the town of Pateros, then Twisp, and stopped for lunch at Winthrop, a touristy westernized town with wood sidewalks.

As we drove, Ann lectured on the landscape like a tourist guide as we traversed past glaciers covered in snow.

It was a delightfully romantic weekend. She dropped me off at my apartment at about nine p.m. "Got to hurry home," she said, leaning over and kissing me suddenly.

"What are you going to tell Derek?"

"I've been on a business trip."

I laughed at the lie, but Ann didn't, almost as if we really had been on a business trip.

"You look depressed," I said.

"Not at all. It was a wonderful weekend."

"You're not sad it's over?"

"Stop it, Jeff. Of course I'm sad, but I'm happy for the time we had."

"I'm always sad when we've been together and then it's over."

"Yes, it is sad, isn't?" She seemed anxious to be agreeable. Then she kissed me shortly on the lips again "Gotta go."

And then she was gone.

17.

Summer arrived, and it was atypically hot, if anything was atypical these days. It went by awfully fast, one day then another, one week followed suddenly by the next. I ran three miles every morning before work and went to the gym Mondays, Wednesdays, and Fridays. I had decided to get into shape, drink less, so on. We saw each other sporadically. Our trip to Chelan had been like a vacation, even though it had been only one night and two days.

Erin continued to come over on occasion, even though she was living with some guy now. She had seemed to reconcile herself to the fact that we were nothing more than fuck buddies. She'd arrive for an hour or two; sometimes she would bring porno DVDs and then was gone like the wind. It was like masturbating.

When Ann and I did get together, my spirits soared with optimism. She could stay away for only so long, I reasoned.

"Isn't Derek the least bit suspicious?" I said one evening as we sat up in bed with our traditional bourbons after making love.

"If he is, he hasn't let on, and if he was, this would have to end."

"Maybe he knows but isn't saying anything."

"I doubt it."

"Maybe he's suspicious but doesn't want to confront it."

"No. Everything's as normal as can be at home."

"When can we get together again?"

"I'll have to let you know."

"Summer will be over before we know it."

"Yes."

"It would be wonderful to get away for a week or two."

"Then Derek *would* become suspicious."

"You can't have another business trip? A convention or something?"

"I'm not going to deceive him."

"What!" I looked at her incredulously and laughed.

"I'm not going to give him any reason for suspicion," she amended.

She seemed to consider what she had said. "I'll let you know."

"About what, a possible vacation?"

"Yes." Then she said, cruelly: "You need to face the fact that we don't have a romantic relationship."

"What was Chelan?"

"Us fucking our brains out for two days."

"That's not true, and you know it."

"If you think otherwise, maybe we should end it."

"All right."

She stared at me. "Your really want to end it?"

"If you really think that all we are are fuck buddies, then yes, I want to end it."

"All right then."

And then she dressed and left without another word. She left her glass half-full. I finished mine and then hers. I fumed and fretted in front of whatever nonsense was on TV.

At work we restricted our communication to business. I was determined to outlast her. It lasted till the end of the summer. Then one day at work we were discussing one thing or another, and then she asked how I was. I was fine; how was she? She was fine as well.

"I miss you," I said.

"And of course, I miss you."

"Then why...oh, never mind." I walked off. I could feel her eyes following me back to my office.

She walked in and sat down across from me.

"Are you dating anyone?"

"No." Which wasn't really a lie, since Erin and I didn't "date."

"Yes, I miss you, Jeff. But you can't seem to get it through your thick skull we will never have a romantic relationship."

"And you can't seem to get it through yours that you love me."

"You need someone to love you, that's the truth, and I'm not that person. I enjoy our time together. I especially enjoy our sex. But I can't say that I will ever love you."

"You can't say that you won't either."

"I can't allow that to happen. I will never leave Derek. You can't seem to understand that." She stood up to leave, and then she turned back to me. "Shall I come over tonight?"

"Let's meet at the Comet."

And then she left.

It was unlikely anyone we knew would be at the Comet. It had become our place to have a beer and discuss matters. Mentioning the Comet meant that I wanted to talk.

I was there first, and by the time she arrived, I had already quaffed an IPA. She apologized for being late. "I had a few items to tidy up."

I didn't know if that was true, but I didn't care; she was here.

"Are you hungry?" I said.

"Starved!"

We were sitting at our usual booth in back, which was dark and relatively isolated; we could talk and not be heard by anyone.

"Haven't see you two for a while," the server said. "Welcome back."

Ann ordered a cheeseburger and fries, I ordered fish-and-chips. Both items were delicious here and deliciously fattening.

"Derek has decided to become a vegan."

"Oh? When?"

"Recently. I told him fine, but it would mean that he become the cook in the household, and that ended that resolution."

I laughed. "Veganism it seems is de riguer these days. Meat is out."

"So is dairy. The industries are freaking out. It's just a phase, like hula hoops and pet rocks."

I laughed. "I think it's more than that. There are ethical reasons behind it as well. Slaughtering and eating sentient beings, the environment, climate change, and all that."

"Yeah, well." She shrugged resignedly.

I knew the topic bored her to tears. I think she just didn't want to face the reality of it.

I said, "I recently read an article that said most of the recycling we sent to China was just tossed into the Pacific."

"What!"

"Yeah, apparently they couldn't handle it all. It means that every time we thought we were doing the diligent thing by throwing an empty plastic water bottle into the recycling bin, it just ended up in the Great Pacific Ocean Plastic Patch. We would have been better off throwing it in the garbage. Anyway, they've stopped accepting it, using Trump's tariffs as an excuse."

"There you go. What's the point?" She shrugged resignedly.

"The point is not to purchase anything plastic to begin with."

"That's impossible."

"I haven't bought any plastic water bottles in years. I have a stainless-steel water bottle."

"Good for you. Can we talk about something else?"

"Such as?"

"Such as, are you through obsessing about me?"

"I'm not through loving you, if that's an obsession."

"That's fine, as long as you realize I'm not through not loving you."

I laughed at her phrasing. She laughed in return.

Ann kept talking about Derek. She and Derek were planning a trip to Africa, a safari. "Derek's always wanted to go."

"When is this?"

"Next winter."

"That's a ways away."

"Yes."

"So, you and Derek are getting along all right these days."

"Yes, of course we are. Always have."

"Even though you're cheating on him."

"If you're going to get into all that again, I'm going to leave… I should go anyway."

And with that, she gathered her things and left, her beer half-drunk.

———— ∞ ————

I seethed all the way home, arriving at my apartment still seething. I decided it was over. Finished. Kaput. I immediately poured myself a bourbon and switched on the TV, too angry to concentrate on whatever crap was on.

As soon as I fell into the sofa, I received a text from Erin. She said she was sitting in her car outside my apartment. *Good,* I texted back, *come on up.*

When I let her in, I was astonished to see she wasn't alone.

"Jeff, this is Alice."

"Hello."

"Hi," Alice said with a shy smile.

Alice was a tall, thin brunette, about thirty-five, I guessed. She was very pretty. I noticed a huge diamond ring on her wedding finger.

"Drinks?" I said.

"Of course," Erin said.

"What would you like?"

"Anything would be fine. Bourbon?" She nodded at the drink I held.

I went to the kitchen and poured three bourbons. I took them theirs and returned to the kitchen to fetch mine. When I returned, they were still standing in the living room. They both had set their drinks on the coffee table. Erin took mine and put it on the coffee table. Then she took my hand and drew me in between them so that I was touching them both on each side of me. She kissed me passionately. Then she turned my head to Alice, and Alice kissed me just as passionately. Then Erin led Alice and me to my bedroom.

For every yin, there is a yang.

18.

This being Seattle in the year 2019, and since I live in the downtown Seattle area, regardless of which direction I head out on my morning run, I invariably encounter homeless encampments, as well as endless construction, or as is usually the case, both. While the construction never seems to end, with giant cranes poking the sky at every street corner looking like a scene from *War of the Worlds*, Mayor Durkan periodically dispatches her goons downtown to clear the annoying homeless encampments, only for them to inevitably return to the same spot as if they had never left, like a car just washed only to be dirty again the next day.

Despite the eyesores, Seattle is booming. And at the top of the heap resides Jeff Bezos, Bill Gates, and other less well-known Seattle area multibillionaires. The wealth of these individuals is so immeasurable that with the least bit of trickling down, there would be absolutely no excuse for thousands of homeless people on the streets. But there they are, nonetheless, an issue that one would think could easily be resolved, but never is.

Somewhere in the middle of this top-to-bottom pyramid resides I, who compared to many, make a decent living. And yet, I cannot afford to buy a house in Seattle, since it would require at least $100,000 down, which I could probably manage if I cashed in my 401K, but then I couldn't afford to finance the rest.

And now, the fact that we literally have a lunatic as president of the United States, the solution to my and everyone else's financial

LOVE AND INFATUATION: THREE NOVELLAS

problems is that much more insufferable. Marx would say that we are living in capitalism's end times, but then, he said that when he was alive, when living conditions were, all in all, worse than they are now. But at least then the ice caps weren't melting.

And thus, dear reader, you can understand why I drink and womanize.

⸺ ❧ ⸺

"How are you and Derek getting along these days?"

"Great. Better than ever."

"I thought you said you two had run out of things to talk about and that you hardly ever had sex."

"I never said that."

"You did."

"Well, if I did, I was probably in a bad mood that day."

We were lying naked in bed, having just made love.

"I wonder what Derek would think about your relationship if he could see us now."

"It's just sex."

"That's what he would say?"

"No, it's what I'm saying. Derek would not be happy, obviously."

Rain pummeled the bedroom window, and it was like going through a car wash. I got up to fetch our bourbons and then returned to bed. We stared at the rain meditatively and sipped our drinks.

When she left, I decided it was over. But I always said that to myself, and then it wasn't over. Weeks might go by, but eventually she would be here.

Christmas came, and other than at the annual party at work, we didn't see each other. I had decided not to get her a gift, but then January 2, at the office, she said she had a gift for me.

"What for?"

"For Christmas. We haven't had a chance to see each other."

"I'm embarrassed to tell you, I didn't get you anything"

"It doesn't matter."

"Yes, it does. I was angry at you."

"All right."

"You aren't hurt?"

"Not at all. I wasn't really expecting one. But I wanted to get you something. It's not much."

It was a Shinola wristwatch. It had a white face with black hands and a brown leather strap. It was the kind of watch she had to know I would appreciate, not inexpensive but not overly lavish either.

I took off my fifty-dollar Casio and put the Shinola on my wrist.

"It's beautiful, Ann. I love it."

She smiled. "It's you."

"It is. Thank you. Now I feel guilty."

"About what?"

"About not getting anything for you, of course."

"Not to worry. I'm sorry you were angry at me."

"Your birthday's coming up. I'll make it up to you."

"You don't have to get anything for my birthday. It's not what we're about."

"Don't say that."

"Why not?"

"Because it's cruel. You got me a nice gift. I want to get you one."

"All right. If you like."

It occurred to me just then that Erin and I had not exchanged gifts, nor had it even occurred to me to get her one. No doubt, it was the same with her. In regard to Ann, it had been conscious, her decision to get me a present; I in turn determined not to get her one.

At my place after work, she announced that she was making some New Year's resolutions to be healthier. "Not drink so much, for one," she said, as she handed over her empty glass for me to refill.

"And what else?"

"Eat better. And go to the gym with Derek. I've gained five pounds."

"I haven't noticed."

"I'm sure you have, but thanks for saying that."

"You look great, Ann."

"You just like curves. You told me that. Which movie star had the ideal body, you once told me?"

"Sophia Loren."

"Oh yeah. I think she looked like a cow, but I'm not a man."

I laughed.

"You work out, right?" she asked.

"A little."

"Run, go to the gym?"

"When I have the time."

"You're an amazing man, Jeff."

I looked at her. I wasn't sure this wasn't sarcasm.

"I'm just a man like any man, not amazing at all."

"I've also decided to end this. It's all part of being healthier, in spirit as well as body."

I took a sip of my whiskey and said nothing.

"You don't believe me, do you?"

"No."

"Then I'll definitely have to do it, to prove a point."

"In the new year, you said?"

"Yes."

"Then we have a little time."

"Don't be a smart-ass now."

19.

Two weeks into January, she showed up at my apartment Saturday afternoon, looking hungover and disheveled. I knew how resolutions worked, and it was why I never made them: you not only broke them but compounded the break rebelliously by drinking even more, eating even more junk food, etc. Although her major resolve to break it off with me did last two weeks; I had to give her credit for that, I thought to myself mischievously.

"We have the weekend," she declared. "Derek's spending a few days with his parents; his mother's ill again."

"Hope it's not serious."

"She's old," she said, fatally. This seemed cold to me.

She was craving fish-and-chips, so we ventured out to walk down to the waterfront. I put an arm around her shoulder and pulled her into me. It was sunny, but there was a harsh chill in the air, and she wasn't wearing a heavy coat. She huddled against me.

We arrived at Ivar's, and she ordered an IPA with her fish-and-chips. Beer seemed an odd choice to me because of the cold weather and that it was only one in the afternoon.

We had a pleasant afternoon in town. We window-shopped, and then I bought her a winter coat at Patagonia.

"You didn't have to do that," she said, walking out into the chilled air wearing it.

"It's my Christmas present."

"Thank you, Jeff," she said, almost officiously, it seemed to me.

"Let's get a drink."

We went into the Virginia Inn, on First and Virginia. It was late afternoon and busy. We managed to find an empty booth.

The waiter was taking his time, and Ann said, "Go fetch our drinks, will you?"

"What would you like?"

But just then the waiter arrived, apologizing. "Someone called in sick and we're shorthanded," he explained.

I ordered a double Jameson, neat, and so did Ann, but with an IPA back.

"Well!" I said.

"I know. Fuck the New Year's resolutions."

I laughed. "Maybe next year."

"It's not funny. I hate myself."

"I'm sorry. Just trying to bring some levity to the situation. I never make New Year's resolutions."

"Good for you."

"Oh, come on, lighten up!"

"Okay." She smiled and put her right hand on my left wrist. It was surprisingly warm. It was making me feel better, but then she had to say it: "What I'm most depressed about is breaking my vow to not see you."

I didn't say anything, and she said, "You don't have to look so smug."

"Do I? I don't feel smug."

"You knew I wouldn't stick to it, didn't you?"

"Yes. I wish we'd made a bet."

"I still don't love you, you know."

I shrugged, and then she said:

"Do you believe me?"

"No."

We laughed. "Okay, maybe I love you a little."

Our drinks came, and Ann surprised me by downing her whiskey in one gulp. She sighed with satisfaction, letting it settle in her gullet, and then took a sip of cold beer.

"There," she said, "that's better."

As I followed her up the stairs to my apartment, she stumbled a little. Inside she paced the room anxiously. I fixed drinks.

"You have to accept things as they are," she said when I handed her drink to her. She sank into the armchair, balancing her drink as she did so.

"All right." I sat across from her in the sofa.

"Will you please stop being so agreeable?"

"Okay."

We laughed.

"I don't want to lose this," she said.

"Why should you?"

"Oh, because," she said, airily.

"What's wrong?"

"What do you think?"

"I don't think anything. I just would like us to have a pleasant evening."

"We're not abiding by the rules," she said.

"What rules are those?"

"Oh, you know, fidelity, loyalty to one's spouse."

"You're loyal to me," I argued.

She started to cry.

"Don't do that, please."

I wasn't about to enable this self-pity, which was no doubt induced mostly by alcohol. She sniffed but stopped crying.

"It bothers you that you love me so much," I said.

She didn't respond to that, though I hadn't asked her anything.

"I'll never leave Derek."

"Yes, you've established that, over and fucking over."

"But you never seem to believe me."

"I'll believe it until you leave him."

"Or break up with you."

I said nothing to that.

In the morning while she slept, I went for a run down to Myrtle Edwards Park and back. It was February, the days getting longer. I wore a T-shirt, running shorts, and shoes—nothing else, though the air was brisk and cold—and a refreshing breeze pricked my face.

When I returned, she was sitting in the living room with coffee. "You're all sweaty," she said, rhetorically.

I pretended to stretch a few minutes and then went in to shower. I could smell breakfast, and when I came out, she was indeed fixing it.

"Shall we go into town this morning?" she said, brightly, energetically scrambling the eggs.

"Sounds like fun."

She smiled as she set my plate down with coffee.

We walked down Third Avenue holding hands. We went to the Seattle Art Museum where there was a Chinese art exhibit, vases made in the Middle Ages, a gold tray made in 1200, a portrait of Emperor Kublai Khan, of the Yuan Dynasty, ink drawings, calligraphy, so on.

We had lunch down at the Market. It was packed, shoulder to shoulder with people. We sat in a restaurant, ordered tuna sandwiches with tomato soup, and stared out at the street.

"I love the city," she said. "But it's become too much."

"Too much what?"

"Too much congestion, too much development, too many cars and people."

"Can't argue with that."

"When Derek retires, we're going to sell our house and move to the Chelan cabin."

"Oh? And when will that be?"

"Not long," she said vaguely.

I changed the subject: "Were you ever in love before you met Derek?"

"For a short time, in college."

"What happened?"

"What always happens, of course; we split up."

"Were you heartbroken?"

"I don't remember. I suppose I was."

"Didn't affect you all that profoundly, apparently."

"What about you?"

"Nothing serious, until now," I lied.

She smiled again, her head cradled in the palms of her hands. She looked out onto the street again.

When we arrived back at the apartment, we lay down for a nap. When I woke, I found Ann in the living room, her legs curled up to her behind, holding a glass of white wine. I filled up my own glass and sat down opposite her in the easy chair. The late-afternoon sun was spilling shadows into the room.

"February is my favorite time of year," she said.

"Really? It's so dreary."

"Not always. Look at it now. Days getting longer. It reminds me that spring is just around the corner, blossoms and fresh starts."

"Then it should be spring that you like."

"No, it's the anticipation of things I like more than the actualization. The anticipation of an upcoming vacation, the anticipation of going to the pub after work on a Friday, so on."

"I see your point, sort of. The anticipation of things always getting better is what you like."

"I suppose, perhaps." She paused to consider this. "Which season is your favorite?"

"I like all seasons. I couldn't stand to live at the equator, for example, where they have summer year-round."

20.

One Monday morning I awoke not feeling myself. I had a sore throat, and my stomach was upset. Nevertheless, I was determined to go for my run and did so after forcing down coffee.

After about a mile, I stopped running. I was suddenly out of breath and could barely breathe. There was a sharp pain in my chest. *Was I having a cardiac arrest?* I wondered. I started sweating profusely.

I managed to return home, trying to run and then having to walk. When I was inside the apartment, I started shivering uncontrollably. I undressed and fell into bed, pulling the covers over me, shivering and then sweating.

I have the flu, I assumed.

I needed to pee, but as soon as I stood up, I got a piercing pain in my chest. I fell back down, but I really did need to pee. I forced myself to the bathroom and sat on the toilet shivering violently. I rushed back to bed and pulled the covers over me, shivering, and then suddenly my body was struck with a dripping sweat. Then my chest thumped violently, and blood rushed painfully to my head.

I opened my eyes. I was covered with a white blanket. There was an antiseptic smell. I was in a bright-white, unfamiliar room. I felt movement to my right and turned to Ann.

"You're awake."

I didn't know quite what to say to that. Of course I was awake. "Where am I?"

"You're in the hospital."

"But...how...I don't remember anything."

"No one from work had heard anything from you in two days, which was unusual. I was worried. I went over to your apartment and found you delirious, your sheet soaked. I called 911. You have pneumonia."

"I do?"

"I warned you about always running in just a short-sleeved T-shirt, you idiot."

"Wait. I'm confused. How long have I been here?"

"Since yesterday. It's a good thing I found you. You nearly died."

Just then Ken sauntered in, an overdone smile on his face.

"Ready to go hit some balls?" he said. "I bet I can kick your ass now!"

"You usually do anyway."

"That's true."

"Have you met Ann?"

"Of course. We've been partying big-time for two days now. We're old friends."

I was in no mood for humor. I felt the need to pee. I started to get out of bed.

"What's this?"

"It's a catheter," Ann explained.

"They found one small enough?" Ken said.

I lay back down and took a breath. I was weak and nauseated.

A man and woman entered. The man began taking my blood pressure; the woman stood over me reading from a chart—my chart—I assumed. "How are you feeling?" she said, not looking at me, combing her hair back with her right hand.

"Never felt better."

Ken chuckled, but the doctor was all seriousness. "You have pneumonia," she declared. I felt she was saying it to herself, not me.

"That's the word on the street."

She looked up at me from her chart for the first time. "It's streptococcus…common but quite serious. If your friend hadn't found you, you might have died."

I nodded.

"But you're young and healthy and should be outa here in a few days. We have you on antibiotics and steroids."

"Hope he doesn't start looking like Arnold Schwarzenegger," Ken said.

The doctor smiled, and all of a sudden that made her attractive. She was midthirtyish, tall and dark-haired and a face clear and distinct. *On another occasion…* I mused.

She left, all three of us appraising her pleasant-looking ass as she hurried out.

"Her bedside manner could use a refresher course," Ken said.

I shivered. "Could you remove this catheter?" I said to the nurse.

"Can you make it to the bathroom by yourself?"

I started to show him, and he said, "All right," before I could. They sure were in a hurry around there.

"Ow." I felt something slip away with a slight painful tweak.

Ken and Ann laughed. The nurse didn't. He left with no further comment.

"Boy, they really know how to have a good time around here, don't they?" Ken said.

"How happy would you be sticking tubes up dicks all day?" I said.

"He probably likes it," Ken mused.

"I don't think that's all he does," Ann said. "At any rate, I see your sense of humor is stable."

Ken and I were laughing like adolescents.

"Jeremy called your parents." Ann said.

"Why?" I stopped laughing.

"Why? *Why* do you think? You almost *died*."

"What did they say?"

"Nothing. Jeremy left a voice mail. Have they called you?"

"If they have, I wouldn't have known, considering."

I looked at Ken, and we started to laugh again.

"Of course. Well, I supposed they'll be in touch."

"I suppose." But I knew they probably wouldn't be.

"I think I'm going to go, honey."

She stood, and Ken followed. "Me too…*honey*."

"Where are you going?"

"We're going to go boink our brains out," Ken said. "By the way, thanks for the use of your apartment, bro."

"Knock yourself out."

We were laughing again.

"Shut up, you two. I brought in some magazines." Ann put a *New Yorker* and *Vanity Fair* on my belly. She pecked me shortly on the lips.

They left. I was relieved when they left. I wanted to be alone. I didn't feel like reading. There was a TV, but I didn't feel like watching TV either. I just wanted to rest. I had never been this sick before. I thought I might enjoy this: just lying there doing nothing.

21.

It took me about a month to return to my old self. I had an unrelent-ing headache and a touch of diarrhea. And strangely, I had lost my sense of taste.

Ann couldn't get away from Derek, and I didn't hear from Erin either. As for the latter, I wondered if she was finished with me. I was beginning to consider the idea of getting a girlfriend—a real girlfriend. I was lonely—and horny. I thought about contacting Dr. Sheffield. I had come to know her somewhat while I was in the hospital and knew she was not married, but of course that did not mean she was unattached. I googled her and could find no contact information other than at the hospital. So, I called and left a message at the hospital for her to call me.

Naturally, it was an office assistant, or someone, who returned my call. "Are you all right?"

"Yes, I'm fine. I just wanted to talk to Doctor Sheffield."

"What for?"

"I wanted to ask her out."

I heard an audible sigh. "We don't have time for this nonsense." She disconnected.

On the same day, Erin appeared.

"Guess what?" I told her. "I've been sick."

"Oh?"

"I had pneumonia."

"Wow. Are you all right?"

"I am now, yes. Though I almost died."

"You poor baby. Can you still get it up?"

"We'll have to see."

We laughed.

"I have some news as well," she said.

"Oh?"

"Yes, I'm getting married."

"Congratulations. Would you like a drink?"

"Does the pope poop in the woods?"

"What?"

"Isn't that funny? You know: 'Is the pope Catholic? Does a bear shit in the woods?' It's a turn in phrase."

"That's pretty good, I have to admit."

After Erin left, Doctor Sheffield called.

"Are you all right?" she said.

"Yes, I'm fine, thanks for asking."

"I hear you wanted to talk to me?"

"I wanted to ask you out."

"On a date?"

"Yes." I heard her laugh.

"All right then."

"All right then."

We made a date for dinner for the coming Saturday.

As soon as I disconnected from Dr. Sheffield, Ann called. She wanted to come over. I wanted to see her, of course, but I was no longer horny, for obvious reasons.

Eight hours ago, I was lonely and horny. Now I was neither. They always seemed to come and go like that, in clusters.

Out to dinner with Dr. Sheffield, or Christine, I asked if she was dating anyone else. She said no and asked if I was. I confessed to her about my situation with Ann. I went on and on, as if she were my therapist rather than a medical doctor. She didn't seem to take offense.

"You like this situation you are in?"

"No. I want her to leave her husband and move in with me."

"From what you've told me so far, it doesn't sound like that is going to happen."

"What about you? Do you want to get married?"

"Eventually. I haven't had time to think about that sort of thing, with my career. I barely have time for myself."

"Ann's husband is always busy too."

"Which is convenient for you two. Does she love you, you think?"

"She says she doesn't, but I don't believe her."

"I think you should take her at her word."

I ordered another bottle of wine.

"You know," she said, after a thoughtful lull in the conversation, "not everyone desires intimacy the way you seem to. Ann probably likes what she has, a husband and a lover. If you can't accept that, you will have to face it. Intimacy scares some people; they prefer to keep their distance. She sounds insecure, if you ask me. I'm not a psychologist, but I know that much about human behavior. I think she uses you as a shield, protecting her from vulnerability. You're an intelligent person. Perhaps she feels beneath you intellectually and doesn't want you to know that. She's afraid of being found out... I'm sort of like that."

"How do you mean?"

"I went all the way through medical school with the thought in the back of my mind that I wasn't worthy. I kept getting good grades and kept being surprised by it. Then I became an MD. I still can't quite believe it. I think it may be a woman thing; women are pro-grammed to feel inferior to men."

"That's changing."

"Somewhat, thank god."

The wine came, and the server poured our glasses.

"I had a relationship with a married man once," she said.

I looked at the server, who didn't react to this bit of news but no doubt was used to hearing this kind of thing.

"Really."

"Yes, while I was in medical school, when I didn't have time for a permanent relationship. It was convenient for both of us."

"What happened?"

"His wife found out. She demanded he end it, and he did."

"How did that make you feel?"

"I didn't care all that much. He was more of a sexual tool than a person I cared about."

I laughed. I thought about telling her about Erin but decided against it.

"If you want to know if she loves you," she said, "break up with her."

"What would that prove?"

"If she loves you, that is when she will show it."

When I dropped her off, I asked if she wanted to see me again.

"I think you need to figure out what you're going to do about Ann first. I won't be second on your list. You have my number. But you have to think about this: if she really loves you, she will leave him for you. And you need to consider this: do you really love her, or do you just need her to love you?"

This bit of insight startled me. When I returned to my car, I turned on my phone. There were several calls from Ann.

When I got home, I parked my car in the underground tenant parking and used the elevator to my apartment floor, as usual. When I got inside, I was startled to see Ann inside.

"Jesus! You scared me!"

"Where have you been?" She seemed frantic.

"Out."

"I can see that. Out where?"

"What concern is it of yours? I had a date."

"A date!"

"Yes, what's wrong with that?"

"Why…" She paused. "Nothing I guess."

"Are you spending the night?"

"Yes, Derek's with his mother. His father died suddenly of a heart attack."

"I thought it was the mother who was ill."

"It happened suddenly."

"His loss, my gain."

"Don't be crass."

I poured two bourbons.

"So," Ann said, "how was your date?"

"It was all right."

"Who was it?"

"Does it matter?"

"Only if it affects our relationship. Are you going to see her again?"

"Actually, I told her about you. She said I needed to figure out what I'm going to do about you before she will see me again."

It felt odd, telling the truth.

"And?"

"And what?"

"Have you figured it out?"

"No, of course not."

Ann got out her marijuana. She usually didn't do that around me, since I didn't care for it, but she did tonight, for some reason.

22.

Ann and her husband went on a two-week vacation, and I didn't hear from her during this period. I thought of texting and then decided against it, mainly because she said not to.

Saturday, Ken and I ran a 10K fun run. With about a mile left, Ken took off ahead of me. I tried to keep up, but was unable to and lost him in the crowd of bouncing heads in front of me. I still had residual sickness from my pneumonia. He had to turn everything into a competition. When I crossed the finish line, the clock read thirty-seven minutes, ten seconds.

Ken approached. "What was your time?"

"Thirty-five minutes, ten seconds."

"That would be impossible."

"Why?"

"Because my time was thirty-six minutes, thirty seconds ."

"Oh, you didn't see me pass you?"

"Fuck you. Let's go get a beer."

That night, Christine called.

"Hello!"

"How are you? I thought maybe you would call me."

"You said not to until I've figured out what I'm going to do about Ann."

"You haven't?"

"Well, no...but I haven't talked to her for a week."

"I'm not sure what that means. But I am free Friday night."

She wanted to see the film *Bombshell*, a docudrama about the way women were treated at Fox News.

At dinner, she asked me what I thought of the film.

"I wonder how factual it is."

"Why would you wonder that?"

"My problem with these films that are supposedly based on true events, they always fictionalize, supposedly for dramatic effects. For example, do you think Ailes was as crazy as that? The film was practically sympathetic to his behavior, as if he had no idea how sick he was and thus no responsibility for his aberrant behavior."

She stared at me reflectively. "You don't think it represented the culture at Fox truthfully?"

"I suppose. But one of the three women characters was fictional."

"She was supposedly a composite of how women in general were, or are, treated."

I nodded. "Yes, I'm sure. I don't know. I can't stand Fox. I never watch it."

"But there are people who do and take it as gospel."

"Yeah, I know. It's crazy. Our whole culture is insane right now. Trump? What the fuck?"

"Taking you to see this particular film was a test."

"A test?"

"Yes, I could never date a right-winger."

"Ah." It occurred to me that Erin and I never talked politics, though I knew she was a right-wing "Christian" conservative. I didn't know for sure if she had voted for Trump; probably, but I hadn't cared. I knew Ann and her husband were Democrats, though not nearly as leftist oriented as I, but I didn't know for sure. "I support Bernie for president, in case you're wondering."

"You're a democratic socialist, then?"

"I'm a socialist. Not sure about the democratic part."

She laughed. "You're not in favor of democracy?"

"Yes, of course. But I think to say it is redundant."

"Redundant?"

"I hate talking politics."

"All right."

"I just think Sanders feels compelled to include 'democratic' to differentiate himself from totalitarian governments that call themselves socialist but are not. China, for example."

"So what?"

"So, I think it's redundant. People shouldn't have to be told that to believe in socialism is democratic. Co-ops are socialistic, but nobody calls their co-op 'the democratic co-op.'"

She stared at me, appearing to think about this. I saw her mind whirring. "Sometimes people have to be reminded how to think."

"Yes, I know."

"You're not part of the 'anyone but Trump' crowd, then."

"Not anymore. I quit voting for the lesser of two evils in 2012. I couldn't take it anymore, all that endless war shit, the NSA, drones, so on… Not in good conscience. Yes, Obama was better than the alternative, but at what point do we move on, for crissakes: the ice caps are melting."

"Who did you vote for, then?"

"Jill Stein."

"Okay! At least I know I'm not dating a right-winger!"

"I try to avoid political discussions on dates."

"It's important for me to know the men I'm going out with."

"I understand. If you want to carry this topic further, do you ever feel guilty about your salary?'

"You want to turn this into a squabble?"

"No. Forget I said that."

"I worked hard to get where I am."

"I know. But there are lots of people who regardless how hard they work remain poor."

"And there are lots of people who have never worked a day in their lives and have loads more money than I."

"Yes, of course. Let's drop it."

"I'm not interested in your salary."

"You don't want to make sure I am acceptable within your social hierarchy?"

"Not in the least."

"Have you heard of a book called *Economy and Ecology: How Capitalism Has Brought Us to the Brink*?"

"No, but I can pretty much tell what it's about from the title."

"If you want to know my political and social orientation, it's pretty much in this book, if you care to read it. I have a copy."

"I don't have time for that kind of thing. I barely have time for the books I *want* to read... So...you won't vote for Elizabeth Warren either?"

"If she's nominated, I might have to think about that."

"Wow."

23.

Ann texted me to say that Derek's mother wasn't doing well; he was taking a leave of absence from work to stay with her until he could make arrangements for a full-time nurse, so we would be able to spend some time together, if I liked.

If I liked?

If remember her saying she and Derek had stood to inherit some money. This "some" money apparently was in the millions. I had said something stupid, like "It's interesting how people with money always seem to find ways to have more money." That hadn't gone over well.

We met at the Merchant's Café for dinner. We had cocktails before dinner, white wine with our dinner, and coffee and brandy after. Then we marched across the street to the J&M Café for more cocktails and carried on a drunken discourse about what, I can't remember.

At my apartment, we sat across from each other drinking bourbon and carrying on with our meaningless banter. We were going to feel like shit in the morning, but it didn't matter now; at the moment we felt great.

"Are we going to carry on like this forever," I said, "just having an affair?"

"Forever's a long time."

"What if Derek were to die?"

"Then...I don't know. I've never given that a thought."

"He's older than you."

"Yes, I guess I figured this would be over by then. Someday Derek and I will be respectable seniors, and you will continue to be a swinging bachelor."

"Is that what I am?"

"Aren't you? I don't know what you do when you and I aren't together. You could be stringing along a whole horde of women, for all I know."

"Are you happy with the way things are?"

"No, I feel guilty."

"Then why don't you stop seeing me or leave Derek?"

She turned onto me a wicked look and didn't answer.

"Forget I said that."

"I think I'll go home."

"Don't be ridiculous. You're too drunk to go anywhere except to bed."

Her phone rang. She looked at it but didn't answer.

"Derek?"

She nodded.

"Why didn't you answer? I don't care."

"He would be able to tell I've been drinking."

We went to bed. As I was about to throw back the covers, she hugged me from behind, her head resting between my shoulder blades. I could feel her stumble, her breathing hard.

In the morning, after coffee and Aleve, she settled into the sofa and returned Derek's call. He mostly spoke, and she mostly listened. I heard enough to make out that Derek's mother was really sick and that he was worried.

When she disconnected, she said she had to go.

"Why?"

"Derek wants me to be with him right now."

"Is he upset?"

"His mother's dying; of course he's upset."

"Do you have time for breakfast?"

"Yes. I need to eat something, or I'm going to be sick."

I scrambled some eggs, toast, and more coffee.

I lay around the apartment. In the afternoon I watched the Seahawks lose to the Packers in a playoff game. Outside it was freezing, and it began to snow. It was very pretty, and I thought I would love to go for a run in the falling snow. But I was too hungover. So, instead, I bundled up and went for a walk. I ambled down to the waterfront and had fish-and-chips and a beer.

I was lonely and couldn't stop thinking about Ann. I couldn't seem to get it through my head that she was never going to leave him. She was over at the mother-in-law's right now for him to cry on her shoulder.

24.

Ann texted me to say that Derek's mother had died. She was taking bereavement leave from work and wouldn't be able to see me for a while.

I called Christine and asked if I could take her out to dinner.

"Are you still seeing that married woman?"

"No." Not this week.

"In that case, why don't you come to my place for dinner?"

I smiled. "I would love to."

She lived in a condo in West Seattle, on the waterfront on Alki Beach. She had a beautiful view of the bay and downtown Seattle. It was windy, and the waves rolled over the boulders and then crashed against the bulkhead, splashing up onto the sidewalk.

After dinner we settled into her sofa with cocktails. We began to make love.

She pushed me away and disappeared into another room, returning with a small package, which she handed to me. It was a condom.

When we awakened in the morning, we began to make love again. She reached into her nightstand for a condom. As the night before, it broke, as I knew it would.

"Shit!" she said, angrily. "You need to wear a size large!"

I knew this, of course, but hadn't said anything.

"I hate those things," I said.

"Of course. I hate them too, but we have to be safe, after all."

"I'm safe."

"I know from your blood work that you don't have any STDs, but that was a while ago."

"I haven't been sexually active."

She studied me. "Well, I guess it doesn't matter at this point, does it?"

"I guess not." I smiled.

She laughed. "You asshole."

She fixed coffee, and after coffee we went for a walk along the bulkhead. It was cold, but the sun reached over the eastern hillside and was warm. She put her left arm into the crook of mine as we walked and talked.

"Sounds like you have a good job," she said.

"It paid most of that ridiculous bill you sent me."

She laughed. "*I* sent you?"

"Do you like being a doctor?"

"I love what I do."

We stopped at the Alki Restaurant for breakfast.

Over breakfast she kept combing her long, dark hair back with her right hand, and it was so thick and wavy, her hand would disappear into the foliage.

After breakfast I felt like we were floating along in a dream back to her condo, her arm in the crook of mine. I leaned over and kissed her.

"I feel very comfortable with you," she said.

I kissed her again.

"I'm horny," she said.

We hurried back.

We spent another day and night together. Sunday she said: "I think I'm going to be sick."

"What? Really?"

"Yes, I really feel like I'm going to be really sick and will have to take next week off." She smiled. "What about you?"

I laughed. "You know, now that you mention it, I think I'm coming down with one serious case of crud, maybe a relapse of my pneumonia. I need you to take care of me."

We laughed.

From her bedroom on her third floor I could hear the waves splashing on shore. They were like a white noise, muffling the occasional vehicle that sloshed by on the wet avenue.

The days were warm, midsixties. In the morning we sat outside on her lanai and observed the bay.

"Look," she said.

A seal had climbed upon a smooth boulder and settled in.

"This summer I'm going to Europe with a friend," she said.

"Warning me ahead of time?"

"No, just mentioning it."

"For how long?"

"A month. In August."

"A female friend?"

"Yes." She laughed, as if how could I think otherwise.

"I'm missing you already."

She laughed. "It's a few months away. Who knows what will happen with us by then."

"Then why did you tell me?"

She looked at me and didn't say anything.

Love follows a pattern. It begins with a powerful physical infatuation. If it continues, it grows into a deep and passionate physical love. This love either passes or settles into a strong romantic love. If the couple is fortunate, this love continues to evolve and stay.

I didn't hear from Ann for two weeks, during which time I fell in love with Christine and fell out of love with Ann.

We walked to Duke's Chowderhouse Restaurant, close to her condo on Alki.

"I'm starved!" she said. "I'm going to guzzle a big mug of beer and then devour a huge salad and Alaskan king salmon!"

From where we sat, we ate, drank, and watched the day slip into night.

In her bathroom later, we stood side by side naked, washing our faces and hands and brushing our teeth—his and hers.

We quickly slipped into bed and wrapped around each other. I was in love but not horny, but the sex came regardless and inevitable.

We lay back, sated.

"I'm going to some friends' tomorrow for dinner," she said, out of the blue.

"Oh? All right."

"Would you like to come?"

"I just did."

She laughed.

"What about you? You sometimes can't tell with women."

She laughed. "I think you could tell."

"Yes, I'd love to meet your friends."

I was allowed to accompany her to "some friends'" for dinner. It signaled to me further basis toward a solid relationship.

The "friends" were Lao and Dexter, a thirtyish gay couple that lived in Capitol Hill in a large 1920s Craftsman. They were a handsome couple and thorough gentrifying, no doubt having displaced a multigenerational black family. They both worked at Amazon. Of course they did.

They hugged me like old friends. They opened a bottle of red wine, and then another before dinner, and another with dinner—which was a vegan lasagna.

"This is delicious!" I said.

"Are you surprised?" Dexter said. "It doesn't have to be loaded with meat and cheese to be good, you know." He seemed annoyed.

"You're both vegans, then?" I said, taking another bite.

"Absolutely!" Dexter said, almost irritably.

For dessert was a vegan chocolate cake, also good, but nothing like Mother used to bake.

The topics of discussion inevitably arrived at Trump.

"He disgusts me," Lao said.

"He's a lunatic," Dexter added.

They looked at me for a response. I had none.

"We feel the same, guys," Christine assured them, and I saw each their shoulders slump in relief.

End of topic. I didn't know who they supported for the 2020 presidential nomination and didn't care. Probably Buttigieg. I felt that Elizabeth taking me here to meet her gay friends was another test.

We drove home through a silver mist. It was February, the month in which all Northwesterners longed for warmer and drier weather, spring. I checked myself, knowing that I was in the infatuation stage of a relationship. Whether this would evolve into romantic love was left to fate.

"Do you ever want to have children?" I said.

"You're planning our family already?"

I laughed. "Just curious."

"I would like to have children someday. I don't know. It's getting late in the day. You?"

"Probably not. It wouldn't be fair to the kid, considering…"

"Why don't you get a vasectomy, then?" This came across as an accusation.

"Because I haven't completely made my mind up yet."

"You need to know…if this is going to continue, I will not tolerate there being other women."

"All right."

"I mean it. I would end it instantly if I thought otherwise."

25.

Ann walked into my office.

"I can come over tonight," she said.

"Is that all you have to say?"

"What else would you have me say?"

"Jesuschrist, we haven't spoken in two weeks. How about 'I missed you, honey,' or at least a simple hello."

"Hello, I need your big cock. How's that?"

She laughed, but I didn't.

"Let's meet at the Comet," I said.

She looked at me. "You want to talk?"

"Yes, we need to talk."

"Uh-oh. All right then."

At the pub after we had settled in with our drinks, she said, "Okay, what is it?"

"What is what?"

"You want to talk, so what is it?"

"It's just that…I've decided to end this."

She stared at me. "End what?"

"The relationship."

"We don't have a 'relationship.' We fuck like bunnies."

"Well, whatever you want to call it, I've decided to end it."

She took a reflective sip of beer. "Okay…tell me why."

"Because I've decided you're never going to leave Derek, and I've had enough."

"I've never lied to you about us."

"I know."

"I thought it worked."

"It did, until it didn't."

"What the fuck does that mean?"

"It doesn't work for me anymore; I want to move on."

"I don't believe you."

"It's true."

"No, I won't come over tonight, but it's not over. You're just in a mood. Tomorrow, or the next day, you'll change your mind."

"No, I'm serious."

"Who is she, then?"

"She's no one. There's no one."

"You're lying. There has to be someone, or you wouldn't be doing this. You can't say you love me and then just end it without there being someone else. I know you."

"No, it's going to be tough, because I love you, but I can't do it anymore."

"I've never felt good about this. I've always thought it was wrong."

"Well, now you can be right."

"It was wrong, but you made me fall in love with you."

"You've always said you don't love me."

"Of course I said that. I was saying it more to myself than you."

"You'll leave Derek?"

"Maybe."

"No, you won't, or you would have by now."

"Let me come over tonight. Derek's out of town. Just one last time."

"One last time?"

"Yes, our last hurrah."

———∞∞∞———

We had one of our most exuberant lovemaking sessions ever. It was almost as if she wanted me to see what I would be missing. And it was true: she was probably the best sexual partner I've ever had.

In the morning she was as jovial as ever, as if things between us could not be better.

"I was serious about what I said last night, you know."

"Yeah, right."

"I mean it, Ann."

"So…what shall we do today?"

"I have plans."

"What plans?"

"Plans that don't include you."

"Let's go to breakfast."

"No, you have to go."

"Oh, all right, I'm going. Can I finish my coffee at least?"

"Yes, of course. But I want you to understand, this is over."

"Uh-huh."

———∞∞∞———

I spent the night at Christine's. I turned off my phone in case Ann tried to call.

In the morning, when I turned on my phone, there were several texts from her:

I hope your happy with yourself. I was surprised at the grammatical error, but then, not so much. *Your an evil person, Jeff. I hope you realize that.*

Jesus.

Another: *I was right the first time. I never did love you and I don't love you now. I in fact was using you for booty calls, for your big dick. You're so proud of that dick, aren't you?*

But it's just a normal dick like everyone else's and so are you.

There were other texts, but I deleted them before reading them. I hoped this would be the end of it.

But they continued. They were like the five stages of grief, at first insisting that it wasn't over at all, and she invited herself over despite the fact that Derek was home; she was willing to take the chance, she wrote. The next text was angry, calling me names. Then she tried to bargain, saying that she would leave Derek and move in with me, even marry me. Then she threatened to kill herself. I ignored them all, just wanting it to be over.

I decided to tell Christine.

"How long has this been going on?"

"What? The affair?"

"Yes."

"It's not going on. It's over, I told you, ever since you. But we had an affair for a couple years."

"And you haven't been seeing her since you and I have been together?"

"No," I lied. I've always been a good liar.

"You're not going to see her anymore."

"No, I am not."

"Because if you are, I can't see you anymore."

"Yes, I know."

The texts continued. She called me "a psychotic, womanizing asshole crazy man."

Ironically, when I masturbated, I thought about Ann calling me these names while I fucked her. I realized I would miss her sexually. I think it was the illicitness of it that excited me, her being a married woman. I treated her like a whore. I would sit in the darkness of my apartment and think about our sex and masturbate.

Maybe I wouldn't be able to give her up.

I panicked.

At work we avoided each other. Then one day she stormed in.

"Why did you do that to me?" she demanded.

"Ann…we had an affair. Now it's over. It had to end sometime; you knew that all along."

"Well?"

"Well, what, Ann?"

"When are we going to get together?"

"You're not going to go all *Fatal Attraction* on me, are you?"

She stormed out.

Epilogue

Christine and I made plans for marriage. Ann harassed me less and less, and soon it was simply the silent treatment. This was fine for me—I didn't want to converse with her anyway—but it also meant that she still was angry and thus still had feelings for me, even if these feelings were to torture me mercilessly followed by a horribly painful death.

Christine went away on a business trip, and I was on my own for two weeks. This was a test. Then I got a text. It was from Erin.

Uh-oh.

The End

THE BEVERIDGE PLACE

1.

His favorite time was morning, when he sat at his desk with black coffee and typed aimlessly into his computer, as if starting out in the middle someplace and gradually, hopefully, developing somewhat of a plot. Out his east window, the March sun appeared over the rooftop of his neighbor's across the street, lighting their garden with a murky fluorescence. Thus, he felt shrouded in a film of security, like a nest. The sparse white clouds hovered around the sun solicitously. The cherry tree out front was blossoming too early. The air was calm like the stillness he felt inside.

The caffeine began to stimulate him; he typed, his fingers just moving across the keyboard.

—————

Jennifer still slept as he got out of his pajamas and into his running clothes.

As he ran, he witnessed the spectrum of colors emerging from the gray morning into spectacular yellows, reds, and greens in contrast to the blue sky. The classic old bungalows that dominated their neighborhood seemed sad and pleading as they faced the encroaching development of the city; the aging cedar shakes, the rotting single-pane-window frames seemed to call out for help. He wished he could.

—————

Later, he and Jennifer walked past Starbucks half a mile or so to their favorite local coffee house, C&P. It was a neighborhood darling to the intellectual composite of the locals; they had musical events, poetry slams, and readings. He had read from his published short stories at the poetry slams and had had readings of his three published books. A young married couple owned the business but not the property, and the owner was threatening to sell the property to a developer. A movement was afoot to prevent it.

They claimed two Adirondacks while Jennifer went inside to fetch coffee and pastries.

He looked over at a young woman, her head bent over a book. He found this refreshing—a book rather than a phone. She was dressed light, as if to surrender to this day of spring fever, her skin white from the winter, her reddish hair braided and adorned with green beads. This seemingly Nordic woman sensed him and lifted her head from her book to look. He smiled. Her stare back was anything but reciprocal. She looked up at Jennifer arriving with lattes and croissants.

Denis had grown his dirt-blondish hair long for the first time in his life and now brushed it back into a ponytail. This was a new look, just for fun, and since he was getting compliments, decided to keep it for now. He wore skinny jeans and a long-sleeved T-shirt from the recently run St Paddy's Day Dash and his running shoes, which were for walking too. He was sort of tall: six-one, which seemed almost average these days. His eyes, he had been told, were green, brown, or blue, depending on the environment—so, hazel. He knew he was good-looking enough, though considered himself no more than ordinary, as he was oftentimes mistaken for someone else. This annoyed him, since he would prefer his look to be extraordinary, different, ugly, even, if it could decree some distinction. Nevertheless, he had a reputation of being attractive to women. He couldn't explain it to himself.

His social community seemed to enhance this mystique. Jennifer had mentioned one night out to dinner with friends how a man with whom she worked told her that his wife was jealous, thinking that he and Jennifer were having an affair. "His name is Homer, and if you saw him, you would laugh. Homer or Denis. Please." Everyone laughed, except Denis, who didn't quite understand. He was almost baffled as to why women were attracted to him.

He and Jennifer had been married three years, his first, her second. They were still honeymooners, as it were, still ensconced in the infatuation stage where sex was omnipresent and problems were nonexistent. He had been carrying on a long-term affair with Pam for ten years, a married woman he had dated briefly in high school but not had actual sex with until ten years later, when they reunited at the ten-year high school reunion. She complained about her husband; he sympathized.

Denis and Jennifer sipped their coffee, nibbled at their pastry, and faced the sun. He again looked over at Helga (he saw her as an Andrew Wyeth painting and fantasized her standing tall and naked at the stream), but she seemed fixated on her book. He strained to see which book it was she was reading but couldn't. Just as well; he would probably be disappointed: J. K. Rowling or some shit.

He had the reputation of somebody whose wife "brought home the bacon," as it were, since his writing paid few bills while she had a generous salary at the Boeing Company.

Jennifer's lover's name was Benjamin, he discovered through early suspicion and then some sleuth work, which wasn't hard, perhaps wasn't meant to be. However, he wasn't to know, he supposed, and decided not to confront her, after all, since bringing it out in the open might mean Donald (Pam's husband) might find out about them as well, of which Pam was adamant that he not. Did Pam love Donald? It didn't seem so anymore, since they had been married for some time and—according to her—seldom had sex, but she needed his financial support.

The more important question for Denis: did Jennifer love Benjamin more than she loved him? This was what mostly kept him awake at night.

They had no obligations of children, only the material things, a house mostly, but that was heavily mortgaged, and a separation would certainly complicate matters. Jennifer and he had been a couple for two years before deciding to get married. Why they decided to make it legal was not so much for religious reasons, though Jennifer had been brought up a Presbyterian. It was simply discussed one night over dinner: why not get married? It was not a philosophical question but a practical one, taxes, etc. So, they did.

And they did love each other; at least, there was no doubt in his mind that he loved her. And she at least appeared to hold a somewhat tender spot in her heart for him as well. They had a lot in common. Neither cared much for sports, though they both worked out. They read similar books. They were interested in the same films. They were both to the left politically, though she seemed more upset about Trump than he did. He thought society doomed regardless: Hillary, Trump, Bernie—the ice caps would melt regardless. At this point, a hopeless sense of doom hovered, all the more reason not to have children.

Nevertheless, couples were everywhere, young and old. It was springtime, and they were emerging from the shadows, parading the streets, parks, beaches, arm in arm. And when these couples split, they quickly found others with which to engage, romantically as well as sexually. To be a couple was natural, part of evolution, in order to promote the species as well as society's mores and survival. And it had survived; human intelligence had rendered a species so successful it was ravaging the planet in one humongous battle for survival, dog eat dog, and this evolutionary progression had resulted in—as far as Denis could see—the most fucked.-up species on

Earth, worse than rats, certainly worse than any particular reptile he could think of. And as such, Denis lived his life under a relentless anxiety from which he could find no relief. No wonder everyone was on antidepressants.

Denis's perspective on the world was from one of superiority, as if he were above it all, psychoanalyzing society as if he were omniscient, when in truth he was as fucked up as everyone else.

As they walked home, Denis looked about his neighborhood as if seeing it for the first time: the single-family bungalows a hundred years old being razed for apartment lofts for two hundred people, it happening so fast he couldn't keep up; the young, burly construction workers howling at one another in Spanish, gulping Coca-Cola, succumbing to the exigency of capitalism, amid bent-over elderly women pushing shopping carts as if hanging on by a thread; the brick mortar of the elementary school badly in need of tuck-pointing. He saw his city expanding from a nucleus like that of a zygote, an expansion of cells with hardly any room to breathe. No one seemed to see that the city was imploding in on itself. The sidewalks teemed with pedestrians feigning their way through life toward some fanciful destination.

2.

Ringing Pam's doorbell for a second time, he worried that she was not home. He hadn't seen her in over a month, and he was excruciatingly horny—for Pam, for absolutely no one else, his head spinning for Pam. Jennifer and Donald were both at work, and thus this occasional opportunity for assignation. She opened the door sleepy-eyed, still in her nightie, as if she had forgotten. He was annoyed for a second, as she paused at the half-opened door, staring at him as if at a complete stranger. She was tall, about five-ten, and they could almost stare at each other eye to eye, as they did in fact do then for one nanosecond. Her eyes were blue as the sky, her mock-blond hair unruly around her perfectly aligned face; she seemed caught in a time capsule traveling at the speed of light, he staring at her beguiled.

As if suddenly made aware of their appointed rendezvous, she grabbed his shirt and snatched him inside, slamming the door.

They were yet to speak. She steered him to bed. They undressed, he as quickly as she, despite her with only a nightie on. Arms and legs entwined, they kissed. He had always believed kissing to be an underrated part of the sex act. The most erotic kiss he had ever seen in film was in *The Thomas Crown Affair*, with Steve McQueen and Faye Dunaway, tongues entwined. To him it was X-rated.

They became lost in lust for each other, writhing in unbelievable positions, the bed on fire with lust and sweat. There was a mindless sensation of weightlessness as he levitated above her and came for thirty seconds or more, then collapsed on top of her, lungs heaving as if he had just crossed the finish line after a 10K. Had she come? He could never tell. He asked her.

"Oh *god*!" she said.

"Sometimes it seems the entire coitus with you is one long orgasm."

She laughed. "I came several times, my love."

He wondered if that could possibly be true. They hugged and napped.

Because of Denis, she had cajoled Donald to move from Kent to West Seattle, where there was less of a house than in Kent, yet it was worth more, so if the affair was to end, they would probably be able to get an even nicer home back in Kent. But who wanted to live in Kent? Not Denis, nor Jennifer, nor Pam, only Donald; it suited his redneck sensibilities.

When Denis had first caught up with Pam at the high school reunion, she was already married to Donald, and Denis was unattached at the time. She had made a beeline at him, leaving Donald behind, befuddled. He could instantly see in those wide, beautiful eyes what her intent was. They talked like old classmates do, intermittently, but she kept finding her way back to him, during which time she managed to slip a piece of paper into his sports coat pocket: her phone number.

A few phone conversations ensued, and then they agreed to meet for dinner. He had to drive to Kent, but like a determined spermatozoon dodging and fighting obstacles toward its frenetic destination, he fought the traffic with one thought in mind: getting laid.

They sat in the parking lot of a Mexican restaurant where he managed to give her an orgasm through her jeans. It was his first hint how easy it was for her to come.

"Your turn," he said.

He had thought a hand job. But she held it like a priceless piece of jewelry, the most perfect geometric structure she had ever seen and thus appropriated it into her mouth; seconds later, she was proficiently guzzling like it was a beer.

"Still hungry?" he said.

What followed was a series of double dates, with his then-girlfriend Ellen, a woman who was serious about him but of whom he did not feel the same.

The passion of his affair with Pam only increased, even after he met Jennifer. The bottom line: it seemed impossible to ever let her go.

3.

One Friday night, he and Jennifer drove across town to attend a party with friends. They were primarily Jennifer's friends; he had not met a one before meeting Jennifer. Santana welcomed them at the door from all four walls. They instantly split in different directions to laugh and greet. He was handed a beer, a bottled IPA. The women were made up to the hilt, their "war paint on," as Jennifer would say. Margaret indeed had hunger in her eyes as she split the crowd en route to him. They put their arms around each other and kissed on the lips, a mite too long beyond a friendly peck, absolutely erotic. He'd mostly had Margaret on his mind all the way over. They'd been flirting with each other ever since Jennifer had introduced them.

"Love you," he said into her right ear.

"Love you *too*," she said back. Then she leaned her torso away from him, and they were still holding on to each other at a forty-five degree angle, staring into each other's eyes roguishly, as if waiting for a more legitimate signal; no more beating around the bush? Her hands began to tickle his sides. His penis began to engorge; she smiled.

"I love your ponytail," she said.

"Thank you."

"It fits you."

"I like your new look as well." She had let her real color grow out, a salt-and-pepper. "It's *very* attractive."

Just then, Jason, her husband, arrived to disrupt this chemistry, like a bubbling scientific experiment tipped over. Denis released Margaret to shake Jason's hand. He nodded meaningfully into Denis's eyes, not with antagonism, just to let him know he understood perfectly. Margaret was voluptuous, and he was pleased to show her off.

The night carried on festively. More alcohol was consumed. The scent of marijuana fueled the air. Couples danced to "Hotel California." He was dancing with Jennifer, and suddenly she broke off to rush over to Jason, almost as if in retaliation, he wondered.

It was all out there, hovering in the air with the marijuana smoke, to later have sex harmoniously. He witnessed Jennifer holding Jason tightly and whispering into his ear. Denis was astonished, and then Margaret grabbed onto him, urging him to dance. A possible swap occurred to him.

And it was true—that night Denis and Jennifer made love with a new ferocity, as if she were Margaret and he were Jason. He wondered if Jason and Margaret were doing the same.

4.

Denis and Jennifer had slept together on their first date. In the morning over coffee, she apologized. "For what?" Denis enquired. "We shouldn't have had sex. I barely know you." "Don't worry about it," Denis said, and she said: "Easy for you to say."

It was the old double standard. Men who succeed in seduction are studs; women who succumb to it are sluts.

As they got to know each other, she later told him she had never expected to hear from him again after that first night. "I thought you'd think I was a slut."

"Aren't you?"

She slapped him hard on the chest.

"I didn't think that at all. I was attracted to you from the start. I assumed you agreed to sleep with me because I'm irresistible."

"Right."

They laughed.

"There you go. And here we are."

He also learned how reticent and serious she was, as if she withheld some horrible childhood trauma in her subconscious that would require extensive psychoanalysis to uncover. An overwhelming silence burdened her, and as time passed, he came to realize that it was unlikely he would ever know her completely.

———⊗⊗⊗———

There was a convenient bar they frequented just one block from their house called the Beveridge Place because it was on the corner of California Avenue Southwest and Southwest Beveridge Place. It became their "watering hole," as it were, and they developed friendly acquaintances there who frequented it. But this particular evening, they saw no one they knew, and they sat talking and sipping their beer.

But then Denis felt a hand on his shoulder, and Jensen sat down next to him with his beer.

"I had one hell of a night last night," he said, with a sigh.

"Good or bad?" Denis said.

"At the time it was good, but it feels bad right now."

"How so?"

"I got drunk and made a fool of myself."

"Oh, well, we've all been there."

"I was talking to this attractive young woman, and we were having a perfectly friendly conversation, but then I leaned into her and said, 'Let your hair down,' since she had it pinned up."

Jennifer stared, and Denis said, "So what?"

"She jumped up and ran off."

"Why?" Denis said.

"Apparently I scared her. I don't know. Later I saw her approaching, and she turned tail again."

"Very strange," Denis said.

"What do you think, Jennifer?" Jensen said.

"I guess she didn't want to let her hair down."

"All she had to say was no. In fact, I just expected her to laugh."

"You took a friendly tête-à-tête with a stranger and turned it into an act of seduction. She didn't like it."

"Oh," Jensen said, pausing, and both he and Denis looked at each other in illumination of this feminine perspective. They laughed.

"Sometimes women just want to have a friendly conversation

and not have to fight men off."

"Yes," Jensen said, nodding as if following along. "I see. If I hadn't been drunk, I doubt that I would have even said it. So now I feel like an asshole. If I saw her this moment, I would apologize."

"At least you didn't grope her," Denis said.

This was in obvious reference to the recent #MeToo movement, in which famous men were being knocked off one by one like at a shooting gallery for inappropriate behavior.

"I've never groped a woman uninvited in my life!" Jensen declared, offended.

"That's good," Jennifer said.

"You know why?"

"Because it's inappropriate?"

"Because I can't think of one reason why any woman would like that."

"However, Jennifer," Denis said, "remember that time we were at the Market downtown and you said, 'Hey!' and I turned to see two huge black dudes walking by and laughing hysterically. You were laughing too. I said, 'What?' and you said, 'That guy pinched my butt.'"

"Well, yes, but that was harmless."

"So, how are we guys to know what harassment is and what is harmless fun?"

"I guess you don't. Caution is probably the best policy."

Jensen was unremarkable in the looks department yet carried this so-far-unobtainable objective of finding the perfect woman of his dreams. He was of average height, well-built from working out, a head of thick brown hair. He had a nose like a bird's beak, long and thin. He had thin lips and crooked teeth. He also had an irresistible charm and was seldom not dating some beautiful woman, the next woman of his self-assured vision.

"Where's Claire?" Jennifer asked.

"It's over."

"What happened?"

"She said the three words for which I simply have no tolerance: 'Get fucking lost.'"

"Just last week you two were head over heels talking about marriage."

"Yes, I really thought she was the one. Apparently I scared her off too, like the woman who had her hair pinned up."

"Perhaps you rush things too much?" Jennifer proposed.

"You think? I should just let things take their natural course and not worry about it?"

Just at that moment he spotted someone and was off like a light. She was Asian, tall and thin and—of course—beautiful. He was talking, and she was laughing.

In a few minutes Jensen was back at their table with his new potential soul mate with fresh drinks.

"Denis, Jennifer—this is Li, spelled L-I."

"Hello, Li," Jennifer and Denis both said at once.

Li had a slight accent, one that one might likely pay no attention to if she were Caucasian, like a dialect from another state in the union rather than a country.

Just then an old friend who had seen better days staggered up. His name was Jim, and he seemed alcoholic, one step way from homelessness. Denis offered to buy him a beer, and Jim accepted. Denis gave him six dollars, enough for a craft beer and a tip. They all hoped that would be it and he wouldn't be back. They all witnessed Jim pay for the beer then pocket the dollar. Also, he returned to their table and pulled up a chair.

"How are you, Jim?" Jennifer said, sympathetically.

"I've been worse," Jim said, ironically, since he probably had not been worse than he was this very moment.

Jim was an anarchist. He even wore a T-shirt on with the old

Edward Abee slogan: "Resist much, obey little." He was one of those who would disrupt women's marches and other demonstrations by throwing rocks through Starbucks windows, and so forth. He was always vaguely lecturing about Marxism but truly held no ideal whatsoever. He was a true anarchist and was simply against everything, the kind of guy when passing a sign that said, "Stay off grass," would immediately stomp all over it simply because it was there, like Mallory's mountain.

"The truth is Claire broke up with me because I confessed to an affair," Jensen said, apparently picking up where he had left off.

"Why did you do that?" Denis said.

"Have an affair or confess to it?"

"Both."

"I had an affair because it seemed the thing to do. I confessed to it to see if she might confess to one of her own."

"Really, Jensen?" Jennifer said.

"Were you suspicious?" Denis said.

"I saw no clues, but isn't everyone unfaithful?"

"No, Jensen, not everyone is," Jennifer said, sighing judgmentally.

Li followed this conversation with an open-mouthed curiosity, as if in study of an alien culture.

It was obvious to Denis and Jennifer that Jensen had sabotaged a relationship yet again.

"If she couldn't forgive me for one slight transgression, then the relationship was doomed from the start," Jensen insisted.

"Maybe she didn't want to marry a cheater," Jennifer suggested. "Maybe she has a history of men being assholes to her."

"Aren't all men assholes?" Jensen said, looking at Denis as if, for example, this were a given.

Denis and Jennifer had already concluded that Jensen sabotaged relationships just when they were becoming serious, that he didn't really want to settle down but was addicted to the infatuation stage of relationships, like a gambler, and when that had passed, it was time to keep gambling.

Seeming to realize that he was ignoring his next possible conquest, he leaned into Li and began talking to her. Li nodded and laughed in response. Denis had the feeling that they were being talked about. And it was true, since he and Jennifer lived their own secret lie.

Just then, at another table, a man stood and started yelling at some poor woman. Then the man stormed off toward the front door but not before stopping at their very table and leering at Jensen for a second. Then the victim of this verbal assault also stood and chased after the man out the door but not before also glancing at Jensen en route.

"What was that all about?" Denis said.

"I haven't a clue!" Jensen declared defensively.

"He stared at you like he wanted to kick the shit out of you!"

"Do you know them?" Jennifer said.

"I know the woman."

At that, Denis and Jennifer immediately understood and sat back in their chairs with a sigh.

Jim ignored all this, sitting glumly with his empty glass. Denis gave him another five-dollar bill, and he was happy again, this time off not to return.

Jensen was one of those types one wondered about how he got through life. He made a good living and apparently was good at his job yet stayed deeply in debt. He seemed to grasp subsistence by living on the edge, with his relationships and his life. His outrageous behavior was complemented by his interminable charm, which somehow managed to carry him further into another calamitous day. No doubt, Claire saw these signals as well. Discovering that he had been unfaithful was the final straw.

Denis, on the other hand, believed that the end of civilization was impending, which included the disaster of love and relation-ships. They were impossible to maintain forever, and all cultural and political mores were in a state of decay, like the last days of Rome, except this time there would be no recovery. He fretted about the inevitable end of his marriage and how to delay this as long as possible.

5.

Occasionally the topic would arise of whether or not to have a child. They both were semi-positive about the idea but going through with it had yet to happen. Jennifer remained on the birth control pills prescribed until they could make a firm decision to proceed. With this they were able to put off the decision indefinitely. They talked about her quitting the pill and placing nature at its will. She didn't like taking them because of the risks, cancer being her main concern.

They also wondered if it was fair to bring a child into this world as it existed today. It was selfish of them, really, when they thought about it. And especially Denis pondered this major interference in their lives, the initial few years of crying and sleepless nights, and then fifteen or so more of inevitable battles with the kid, and then paying for college. And there was the time Jennifer would have to take off from work, which would further compromise their already strained financial situation.

So, for now, Jennifer remained on the pill.

───❈───

The next time he ran into Jensen at the Beveridge Place, he excitedly told Denis that he and Claire were back together.

"What happened?"

"I suggested we get married, and it seems that was the ticket! Now she's ecstatic!"

"Do you want to get married?"

"No, but I can't live without her."

"Did you ever hook up with Li?"

"Li?"

"That Asian girl."

"Oh, her. Yes, but that's over now, obviously."

Denis laughed, and Jensen looked back with an expression of total naivete.

"Why can't you two just live together?"

"She refuses, unless we're married."

"She's religious."

"A *Catholic*." He expressed this as if of all the religions in the world, this one was the most caustic.

"Who's going to live with whom?"

"Her parents are going to give us the down payment for a house as a wedding present."

"So there's money in the family."

"Tons, apparently."

"You're a cad."

"Oh? Why?"

"You'll have to change your ways, you know."

"Change my ways?"

"You know what I mean."

"How so?" He looked innocent as a lamb about to be slaughtered.

"You will have to be more responsible."

"Well, yes. Of course."

"And women?"

"I'll give them up!" he announced, as if to quit smoking only after discovering he had lung disease.

"You guess?"

"No, I will. I'll have to, absolutely."

"You sound like Jim when he talks about giving up alcohol."

"You don't believe me?"

"I believe you mean it."

Speaking of the devil, just then Jim drifted in and came to them like a dog following a scent, standing over them with a mournful look.

Denis gave him a five like a biscuit to a dog, and he snatched it and was off to the bar to order a beer. He returned with a pint and pulled up a chair. They watched as he put the schooner to his lips with both hands shaking.

The main reason Denis was even here was because he and Jennifer had gotten into a quarrel. She was in one of her "moods," and when she was like this, he wanted to be nowhere near her. She would complain to him for the most insignificant reasons, such as leaving the refrigerator door open a few seconds too long, for breaking a branch off one of her precious bushes out in the garden, for leaving a coffee stain on the kitchen counter, not placing his toothbrush back to its prescribed place, so on. She entered stages of deep depression over nothing.

He returned to the bar to order another IPA and realized he was standing behind someone he knew, Mayra. He playfully tapped her opposite shoulder from where he stood, and she said, "Hello, Denis," without looking at him, obviously already having been aware of his presence. "Excuse me," she said, moving around him without looking at him to take a seat on a stool at the bar with her book. This indifference to his presence disturbed him.

What did he do? he wondered, since he must have done something.

Back at the table, he said to Jensen, "Did you see Mayra?"

"No, where is she?" He looked around.

"She's sitting on a stool at the bar."

"Ah."

"She treated me like a pile of dog shit around which she had to step."

"You are."

Jim roared with laughter. "You are!" he repeated.

Jensen was off to talk to her. A minute later, he was leading Mayra back to their table.

"I'm sorry, Denis. I didn't mean to appear dismissive. I've had a bad day."

"I'm sorry."

"No worries, it's just work."

More pints were consumed, and the mood at the table became festive.

Which didn't help Jennifer's mood when he arrived home about ten p.m., when she was heading up to bed.

"How much did you have to drink?" she said.

"I'll quote Dylan Thomas's last words: 'I've had eighteen straight whiskeys... I think that's a record.'"

6.

Denis found it interesting that political commentary at the Beveridge Place was decidedly to the left. The fact that they didn't live in Bumfuck, Arkansas, was one palpable reason, but nevertheless, the rhetoric was for the most part liberal. That liberality, however, ran the gamut, in Denis's mind, from Clinton/Obama to Marxism, which left a gorge in between for raucous argument. Occasionally, someone might say, "I don't talk politics," which meant one of two things: he/she was apolitical or a Trump supporter.

The topic was becoming tiresome to Denis, the Trump buffoonery carrying determinedly on despite its the absurdity. Denis had read *Fire and Fury*, the nonfiction book by Michael Wolfe, and at one point, Wolfe had said that those surrounding Trump held him in a sort of awe, almost as if he was magical, since despite the fact that he was of less than average intelligence, continuing to spout the most ridiculous statements in his rhetoric and his illiterate tweets, he managed to carry on. Denis supposed there were other leaders as ridiculous, Nero, for example, but none he could think that were elected to power. But then, he wasn't really elected, was he, since democracy didn't really exist in America anymore, if it ever had.

He was discussing this phenomenon with Jensen and Claire, and they nodded their heads in agreement.

"Have you seen Jim?" Denis said, thinking that Jim should have come stumbling into the bar by now; suddenly it occurred to him that he hadn't lately seen the one of them who was about as far to the left as one could go on the political spectrum.

"No, I haven't," Jensen replied, with a scan around the bar, as if he too was suddenly made aware of their friend's absence and, with it, their complicit worry.

"You two should forget about Jim," Claire said.

"Forget about Jim?" Jensen said back to his betrothed in astonishment.

"You're just enabling him, buying him drinks all the time."

"He could be in a gutter, dead!" Jensen shot back, protectively.

"And that would be his choice. He's made his own bed."

"In the gutter?" Jensen said, turning to Denis, and they both laughed.

"Now you're making jokes. He's a sad case, but there's nothing we can do about it. He has to face his own demons."

"So, you wouldn't give your spare change to a panhandler because you would know he's just going to buy alcohol with it," Denis said.

"I would not. You would?"

"I would and do."

"Why?" the woman who had more money she knew what to do with said.

"I'm not sure. I guess I think it doesn't hurt to give the poor sod a bit of brief comfort."

"And that's what you do with Jim."

"I never really thought about it before, but I guess that's it."

"Jensen?" She turned to her fiancé. "Oh, never mind, you throw money around like there's no tomorrow anyway."

Denis wanted to ask about their impending wedding, but they didn't appear to be in the mood to discuss the topic.

Jensen and Claire had previously experimented with an open relationship while agreeing to remain faithful "spiritually," in other words, refrain from falling in love with someone else. Claire ended the experiment when she realized that Jensen loved all women, perhaps not always sexually, but certainly "spiritually." It then became necessary for Jensen to engage in his extracurricular activities on the sly. This didn't work either, since Claire of course found out. So now she demanded fidelity through the institution of marriage.

7.

Though Denis didn't make enough money from his royalties to pay the bills, he was somewhat of a celebrity among the literary crowd. Everyone knew him, especially in the Seattle area. He constantly received flattering emails from fans, usually with an attachment of some prose asking him to read it and possibly send it on to his agent or publisher. He ignored them, not even giving them a chance, even if their work might be good; he was not an agent or publisher, after all. Do it the hard way, as he did.

Sometimes he would get a negative email, such as, "I read your book and I don't understand what all the excitement is about. You suck. I write better than you." Ironically it was these he sometimes responded too, usually with some polite comment like "I'm sure you are. If you're not 'into' my book, do what I do when I don't like something: put it aside."

He knew local writer Sherman Alexie, had never liked him, nor did he care for his writing, which he found boring and sophomoric, and yet Alexie treated Denis as an underling in the world of literature, he himself a star. The recent allegations of sexual misconduct didn't surprise him, considering the current atmosphere, and Alexie had been known as a womanizer. The discovery of his inappropriate sexual aggressiveness didn't surprise him either, because he was simply one of those particular kinds of narcissists who felt entitled.

The one who held absolutely no interest in Denis's celebrity, or his writing, was Pam. She hadn't read a word of his books and, furthermore, could not have cared less. They never discussed literature, politics, art, or anything outside the topic of sex. Their relationship was based solely on the carnal. Through their necessity of secrecy, they developed an affinity for having sex at inappropriate places: in one or the other's vehicle, in dark alleys, in parks, so forth. One time she was giving him a blow job in Lincoln Park, and some guy venturing off a trail came upon them. Startled, the poor dude turned tail and frantically pushed back through the same bushes from whence he had come.

Another time they were in Camp Long looking for a private place in which to fuck and he became so dizzy with desire for her, he had to sit a moment. He was literally about to faint. Pam thought this hilarious.

Right now he was on his morning run making a beeline to her house with this same urge, half a hard-on the entire way, running seven-minute miles.

She told him she would leave the door unlocked. He arrived, his dick guiding him directly to her bedroom like a dog scenting a bitch in heat, where she lay in bed waiting, just as anxiously. A minute later, as they were in the midst of lovemaking, suddenly Pam gasped and stood straight up.

"Donald's home!" she declared and rushed out the door,

"What the…" Coitus interruptus.

This had never happened before. She had always insisted it was safe because Donald *never* came home early; he was too anal about his attendance.

For a moment, Denis panicked, not knowing what to do. Then he gathered his senses, as well as his clothes, lifted open the bedroom window, frantically cast his clothes out, and followed, squeezing his lanky body through the window and down onto the spongy garden. He gathered up his clothes and ran around to the side of the house to put them on. He felt a presence and looked to his left where he saw the neighbor woman looking out at him from her window, open-mouthed, with a delighted expression.

As he put on his clothes, he listened to Donald pounding on the front door. When Pam opened it, he said, "Why is the door latched?"

"I always latch it when you're gone."

"Why are you naked?"

"I was getting ready to shower."

He heard the door close.

Denis finished putting his clothes on, ran across the front lawn, jogging home, catching his breath.

8.

One sunny Monday afternoon, Denis and Pam decided on a local popular restaurant for lunch. Once inside, he spotted Jennifer sitting opposite her lover Benjamin in a booth by the window. At least he assumed it was Benjamin, since he had never met the man nor had he seen any pictures of him. He considered leaving but then decided it would be amusing to stay. They were escorted to a booth.

"Jennifer's here with her boyfriend," Denis said.

"What? Where?"

"Don't look. They're sitting in a booth at the front window."

"What are we going to do?"

"Eat."

"Oh my god!" She laughed at the irony of it.

After they had ordered, suddenly Jennifer was standing in front of them.

"Hello," Denis said. "You look good," he said, as if they hadn't seen each other in ages.

She put her hand straight out toward Pam to shake. Pam graciously took it.

"I'm Jennifer."

"Pam."

"Why don't you join us?"

Pam looked at Denis, and he shrugged back. "Okay," he said to Jennifer.

They followed her back to the booth and sat down opposite

them. Pam and Denis were introduced to Benjamin. He was a handsome man, no surprise there, a lean, muscular look, receding salt-and-pepper hair, and a rugged, unshaven look, as was the style. He had strikingly black eyes. It occurred to Denis that he was the exact physical opposite of him. He pondered the relevancy of this.

They chitchatted about inane subjects, the weather, politics (Benjamin was a liberal at least, thank god), played with their meals, drank their coffee, and then Jennifer said:

"Are we going to talk nonsense, or are we going to address the elephant in the room?"

"Where?" Pam said, looking for an elephant. Everyone laughed.

"What is it that we should talk about, then?" Pam said, somewhat cuttingly, Denis felt.

"Does your wife have a lover, Benjamin?" Denis said.

"Not that I am aware."

Denis was impressed that he didn't end his sentence with a preposition. "Does she know about Jennifer?"

"I think she suspects something. She hasn't brought it to my attention, however."

"Do you have other lovers?"

"Okay," Jennifer said, "that's enough."

"You were the one who wanted to broach the subject."

"Well, now that we have, let's just get along, okay?"

"Be friends? Go on double dates?"

"Don't be an asshole now," Jennifer warned.

Denis realized he was indeed being unfair. Was he jealous? "I was just teasing."

"You were being sarcastic."

He nodded. "Perhaps a little. Sorry."

Pam laughed. She was enjoying the dynamic between her lover and his wife and her lover.

"You're very attractive, Pam," Jennifer said.

141

"Thank you, and so are you."

"I think we can all agree that we make a handsome foursome," Denis said, and they all laughed. "Why wouldn't we?"

Just then, they all turned to look at a lanky, wretched-looking character staring in at them from outside. He looked like a homeless person, with a worn, pitiful expression of hopelessness.

"It's Jim!" Jennifer said to Denis.

"Who's Jim?" Benjamin said.

Just then, Jim turned to the left and was gone.

Denis slid away from the booth and ran outside. But he couldn't see him; he had disappeared.

9.

For some reason, Denis had lately been thinking a lot about his father, who had died at the age of fifty-five from a heart attack—or heartbreak, he wasn't sure. He had always been in business for himself but was never a success at whatever endeavor he pursued. He had a steadfast belief in the American myth that anyone could become a success in one's life if only one made the effort. He tackled life like climbing a mountain, only to find after struggling to the top, disappointment. But his resolve was never-ending, until at last the disappointments were too daunting, in his career, and in his marriage.

He had married a beautiful woman, especially beautiful to have married a man of such modest means, since she too was waiting for the success his father always promised but never delivered.

She had affairs. His father knew about these affairs but, as far as Denis knew, said or did nothing about them. To add salt to the wound, these affairs were always with men who were more handsome and more successful than he was, everyone respected in whatever field they were in, whether medicine, law, or engineering—in the latter of which, Denis's father had a degree.

His father approached each endeavor with a positive energy that was not understandable to Denis, given his history. And then after each defeat, he fell into a long weary depression where he could virtually do nothing, not even mow the lawn.

His mother now was sixty-five, remarried to a man who had been one of her lovers, living in a retirement community in Scottsdale, Arizona. He occasionally gave her a call, and she to him, but seemingly as a familial obligation from which ensued small talk and a quick disconnect. There had never been much love expressed between the two; he had always been angry with her, for obvious reasons. His older brother was more forgiving and communicated with her more often; it seemed, to Denis, almost Oedipal.

Denis hadn't grieved at his father's funeral, and he wondered why; did he lack empathy? Was he a narcissist? Had he not loved his father? Or his mother? Peter was the one who cried his eyes out; he had commiserated with his father's optimism and his setbacks, even following him into an engineering career, though in his case, it was with an employer, who provided him with a decent salary and the benefits that accompany it, health insurance, vacations, so forth.

Denis worried that he lacked compassion whatsoever, other than his need for female company and its physical release. If Jennifer were to die, he would waste no time searching out a replacement. Grief to him was seeking out comfort in sex, a sort of maternal comfort. It wouldn't take a psychiatrist to understand that he pursued women to compensate for his mother's inattention. Talk about Freud, it was almost an Oedipus redundancy; his lack of grief at his father's funeral almost as if he had taken his father's eye out and killed him himself. Unlike Peter, Denis had always been furious with his father's failures, wanting to tell him to "get a fucking job!"

Despite that, Denis had always had a fanatical need for approval from both his parents, and when not receiving it (his father was always jealous), got angry. His mother looked on Peter's success stoically, as if expecting no less and, more likely, much more.

Summer had engulfed the city, and people poured onto the streets hungry for sun after nine months of hibernation. The usual attendees at the Beveridge Place now gathered outside on the patio surrounded by greenery, sun, and shade. Denis carried his pint of beer outside to join the others. He nodded at acquaintances, found a seat by himself. He was sipping a beer, luxuriating in the sun; who could want more out of life?

Denis looked over and was shocked to see one of his mother's former lovers, a neighbor of his parents at the time, someone he had not seen since that time, and now was shocked at how much he had aged. Of course, now that he thought about it, he had to now be around seventy, since he was older than his mother. He had been the Lothario of the neighborhood and his affair with his mother hardly a surprise to anyone. He was mesmerized by this once handsome, now emaciated face, his once lucent blue eyes buried within folds of loose skin, the skin on his arms nearly translucent.

He waved at Denis with a smile, and Denis waved back. He then stood, his once imposing six-foot-four no taller than Denis now, and carried his beer over to Denis's table.

"Hello, Denis," he said, sitting down opposite him without an invitation.

"Hello, Mr. Halston."

"Call me Hal," he said.

Denis regarded Hal, leering at the rivulets of sagging skin and searching for the man with whom his mother had fallen in love. He tried to imagine them naked, entangled in sheets, and could not comprehend it. Despite the history, he still somehow envisioned his mother the Madonna.

"How's your mom?"

"She's fine. She's remarried and lives in Arizona."

"Ah. I never got to tell you how sorry I was about your father." And why should he? Denis wondered. "Fifty-five. Too young."

"Yes."

Denis thought this eerie, surreal, his mother's former lover sitting down with him as if they were longtime friends, when the words spoken between the two had already been more than ever said to each other, which was none.

"And how is Mrs. Halston?"

"She's passed." He sighed with resignation at the sad passing of things.

"I'm sorry."

"Yes." He expressed sincere pain, as if still grieving. "I loved your mother very much," he said, ironically, as if it was suddenly Denis's mother they were talking about, not Mrs. Halston. "I hope she's happy."

"She seems to be."

"That's good." He nodded.

Hal talked, and as he did so, seemed to become more animated, perhaps from alcohol, perhaps from the piling of sentences on top of one another, as if it weren't Denis he was talking too, just someone there to listen.

"Can I buy you another beer?" Denis said, standing, waving his empty.

"Oh goodness no, one's more than enough for me these days." And he rubbed his gaunt belly with a pained expression, as if there lay the arbiter for his imposed moderation.

Denis went to get another pint, taking his time, hoping that Hal would be gone when he returned, since he was in the mood to relax by himself in the sun with a beer, not engage in conversation with one of his mother's old fuck buddies.

But alas, it was not to be.

"Your mother was a beautiful woman," Hal carried on rhetorically as soon as Denis sat. "I wish I had met her before your father had."

"Why didn't you two leave your spouses and marry each other?"

Hal stared at him. "Do you want to hear a story?"

Denis thought: *No*, but shrugged his okay.

"We had once conspired to leave our respective spouses and run away together."

"Really?" Denis was now all ears.

"Yes. My wife had no idea I was having an affair and so was shocked with the news. She watched in disbelief as I carried luggage out to the car. Your mother and I had agreed to meet at a motel and stay there until we could find more permanent living arrangements."

He paused, and Denis said, "And?"

"She never showed."

"What?"

"I waited in the motel room for hours. Finally, I called her from the motel phone. Your father answered. I asked for her. You know what your father said?"

"No, I don't."

"He said, 'She doesn't want to talk to you, Hal. It's over.'"

"Are you kidding?"

"I am telling you the god-awful truth. I had to crawl back home and grovel for forgiveness."

"Oh my god. My mother is a bitch!"

"No, she isn't. I've long forgiven her. Believe it or not, your mother loved your father very much."

10.

Denis assumed for convenience's sake that he and Jennifer had an open relationship. Though the agreement they had was—at least verbally—restricted to each other's lover, he presumed the moral and legitimate right to engage in the occasional tryst if it were to happen, assuming in turn that Jennifer was free to do the same. Whether she had or not he did not know and did not want to know, since it would complicate what they had agreed upon verbally and open the subject up to further negotiation, which he preferred to avoid.

And so, in this constant state of desire coupled with almost a sense of duty to his gender, he had decided to act on his flirtation with Melissa, another regular at the Beveridge Place. She was a real estate agent, single, and thirty-one years of age. Because the attraction they felt for each other was obvious to everyone else, he felt that his marriage was an impediment to them moving forward. So, one evening as just they two sat across from each other at a table, he told her about his marriage.

"You have an open marriage?" she said, expressing surprise.

"Yes."

"Why are you telling me this?"

"Why do you think?"

She took a sip from her white wine while staring up at him searchingly. "You want to have an affair."

"Yes."

Melissa had long, lustrous, brown hair that stretched halfway down her back. She stood about five-foot-three, maybe 130 pounds, not thin, but enticingly healthy, with sexy curves, large breasts and hips. She had a prominent nose, which in Denis's mind added a unique charm to his erotic attraction.

There was a pause in the conversation, as if Melissa was considering her options.

"I like you, Denis."

She said nothing further, and Denis said, "And of course I like you."

"And that's the point."

"The point?"

"Because I like you, if we were to have an affair, I might fall in love with you. If you were single, as I am at the moment, that might be fine. But you're married. And I like Jennifer too."

Nonetheless, at her house, he followed her to her bedroom, where there they hurriedly undressed before either one of them had time to change their mind.

Denis had always marveled at the exclusivity of women, which of course extended to the erotic.

"You didn't come," he said, somewhat slighted.

"No. Sometimes I don't. Sometimes I can't even make myself come. It's all right. I enjoyed the lovemaking nevertheless."

He nodded, up on one elbow, observing her nakedness, perfect in this distinctiveness as well, the robust foundation of her white breasts, the smoothness of her flat belly, the thick foliage at the V between her thighs.

"Thanks for not shaving," he said.

She laughed. "Really? I'm very hairy."

"Yes, I like it."

"You like it! Haven't bothered lately because I haven't been having sex."

"Well, don't do it for me."

"What about my armpits?"

"Personally, I wouldn't care either way."

She laughed. "I will continue to shave my armpits."

"All right."

With that, he felt she had granted permission to continue their affair despite her worry that she might fall in love with him.

Further experimentations with his new lover resulted in occasional success with the orgasm issue. As couples do, they figured it out. And surprisingly—he felt—that success occurred from the (perhaps unfairly) slandered missionary position. Hovering over her, he watched as she shut her eyes as if to concentrate, her teeth clenched, anxiously contorting against his thrusts, even one time culminating in a rare simultaneous climax.

During this period of the current #MeToo movement, perhaps for the first time in history, men as a unit were academically considering how they had treated women and whether it had been proper or not and whether or not the behavior should continue. Denis certainly had. He had recently been making an effort to not be so ostentatious in his observation of women, not just beautiful women but all women, young, old, fat, thin, beautiful, or otherwise. He had until now assumed that women liked the attention; otherwise, why would they dress and make themselves up the way they do? But now he wondered if perhaps women didn't like men ogling them all the time regardless.

He remembered his mother once saying just that—that she was tired of men ogling and propositioning her all the time, but then when it suddenly stopped, she admitted that she missed the attention. She realized it was at this moment in her life that she had stopped being a young and desirable woman and as such, grieved its loss, despite detesting it while it was going on.

He began to think of his gender as primitive, still swinging from their tails tree to tree in quest of some female to satisfy ever un-questionable sexual needs. He was no different, as he followed each woman down the street wondering what those tempting derrieres looked like under those tight yoga pants.

One time he was sitting in a Starbucks with his book when he happened to look up as a foursome of fourteen-year-olds (or so) en-tered and got in line. One of the parties in particular got his attention with her alluring breasts and hips contained within these same cur-rently popular yoga pants. She caught him looking up at her from his opened book, and she smiled. What did this mean? She kept glanc-ing at him in this flirtatious manner. After they had purchased their sugary, caffeinated drinks, he followed her out the door, and just as they were about to disappear at the window, she bent backward and cast him one last, quick, come-hither look.

She clearly liked the attention from this old man, no doubt hav-ing just recently become aware of her bourgeoning body and its ef-fect on men. He realized it possible she may never again look as enticing as she did this very moment, ironically, since she had been declared unsuitable by social mores and arbitrary legal restrictions.

Floating along obliviously in this infinite sea of women, on the streets, in the cafes and bars, ever alert for opportunity, he knew the number of women with whom he had had sex was a grain of sand compared to the nearly four billion women there were in the world. And life was so short; his window of opportunity would quickly de-crease with his increasing years, leaving him with a nearly desper-ate need to take advantage of what fleeting moment remained. He thought of the old bumper sticker, "So many women, so little time."

Artists have attempted to capture this brief moment for thou-sands of years, in portraits, pictures, statues, and photographs. In this entombed fantasy, Marilyn Monroe will remain forever beauti-ful. On TV it was obvious to viewers that being beautiful was a cri-terion for employment as a news anchor or journalist. TV and movie producers have known this since the beginning, but now would be unable to make use of the infamous casting couch because of that fucking #MeToo shit.

———— ∞∞∞ ————

One Friday night at the Beveridge Place, Denis queried Jensen about the upcoming wedding, twice, and twice Jensen avoided the question. Then, after the third inquiry, Jensen said finally:

"Can you imagine spending the rest of your life with the same woman, the only woman you will ever be with again?"

"Uh-oh."

"No, no, the wedding's still on. I've just been ruminating life and so on."

"Of course you have. You need to decide, Jensen."

"You wake up every morning next to the same woman you woke up with the day before, and all the days before that, for years, you both have bad breath, you go to the bathroom like you do every morning, make disgusting noises shitting and pissing, brush your teeth, go down to have coffee, then off to work—and up the next day going through it all again, until your retire at sixty-five, when you have all this free time on your hands but can't get it up anymore."

"I understand absolutely."

"You're married. How do you do it? Oh, never mind, I know how you do it. You think I haven't noticed you and Melissa?"

"Is it that obvious?"

"Of course it is, dumb fuck."

"Well, then, there's your answer."

"I'm afraid Claire would not understand."

"Then you will have to be surreptitious."

"What's that mean?"

"You'll have to be especially secretive."

"You know that works for only so long."

Denis nodded. "I suppose you're right. I don't have any answers for you, dude."

"I do love her."

"I know." Denis nodded.

"And I'm not married yet!"

"No."

"So, let's go find some women."

"What? Where?"

"Downtown?"

"All right."

He followed Jensen out the door and down the street to his car, a BMW convertible. It was warm, and the top was down. The car soared over the West Seattle Bridge at sixty miles an hour, to the viaduct, the counter wind breezing through their hair, turned off onto Seneca Street, and then right toward Pioneer Square. He miraculously squirreled into a parking spot by the Good Bar.

Inside, Jensen immediately zeroed in on two women sitting at a table, one blond, the other brunette. The blond wore a full-length dress that barely touched her thighs. The brunette wore a see-through top and ripped jeans.

They sat down across from them, and Jensen said: "What are you girls drinking?"

They told him, and Jensen flagged down a server, ordering four drinks.

They chitchatted, and when the women had downed their drinks, they excused themselves.

"Where ya goin'?" Jensen enquired.

"Outside to smoke."

"Oh."

When they were out of sight, Denis said, "Smokers?"

"Who gives a fuck. We're not going to marry them. Which one ya want?" Jensen said.

"I don't care. Either one."

"I like the blond."

"Okeydokey!"

Once they returned, four fresh drinks were on the table. Then the blond, whose name was Sara, said:

"I don't think you guys get it."

Denis and Jensen looked at each other.

"Get what?" Jensen said.

"We like you guys," she said, shrugging. "But we're not free."

"You mean," Jenson said, unsure, "you have husbands? Boyfriends?"

"No. You're still not getting it. There's a price."

Denis and Jensen raised their eyebrows at each other with this enlightening bit of news. They were right: they had not got it.

Denis had never been to a prostitute, for two reasons: one, he never had needed to, and number two, the idea had never appealed to him.

Denis drained his drink. "All right, girls. Have a good night."

He stood. Jensen hesitated then also stood.

Outside, Jensen said, "Let's to the J&M."

"No," he said, shaking his head and sighing. "It's late. I'm tired."

"What a fucking waste of time and money this shit was."

"Ya win some, ya lose some. It's prob'ly for the best, anyhoo."

"Let's go to the Beveridge Place," Jensen suggested.

"For a change."

"I still feel like drinking."

Back on the viaduct, the wind felt even freer and fresher against their faces. On the West Seattle Bridge, they cruised past other vehicles, eighty miles an hour. The hillside ahead was congested with homes and evergreens. They passed a bare spot on the hillside where a homeowner had clear-cut city property for a view and had got caught.

Jensen pulled into Denis's driveway, and they marched up to the bar.

11.

It was Jensen's wedding day. He looked handsome and sophisticated in his tux, and other than his conspiratorial shrug at Denis, glowed with happiness (and perhaps alcohol). He appeared to no longer doubt his decision. At any rate, it was too late now. He shook Denis's hand and kissed Jennifer on the cheek.

"Love you guys," Jensen said.

"I'm so happy for you two," Jennifer said.

"I'm so in love," he insisted, as if to convince himself.

"That's probably a good start," Denis said.

"Fuck you."

Most of the older people present wore summer suits, some more business casual, while most of the younger people seemed dressed like a night at the Beveridge Place. Denis wore dirt-brown casual slacks, black boots, and a black sports coat, no tie. Jennifer wore a long, flowery, celebratory dress that hugged her entire body enticingly. He watched the ridiculous old fucks ogling her.

They saw a few people they knew, most of them they did not know.

"I wonder if Jim will come," Jennifer said.

"I doubt it. No one's seen him in a while."

"Aren't people worried?"

"Yes, I've been thinking of going to his apartment to check on him."

"Good idea."

They were introduced to Jensen's parents, Mark and Ruth, who looked like—and probably were—old hippies, Mark wearing a plaid shirt and a black leather vest and jeans, his white receding hair in a ponytail as if he'd had it since the sixties, which he'd likely had, and a huge belly hiding his belt. Ruth's hair was likewise white, in braids, and she wore a paisley dress. She wore numerous silver necklaces and bracelets that seemed to weigh down her tiny, emaciated-looking body; she couldn't have been five feet tall and a hundred pounds, contrasting to her massive six-foot-something, three-hunded-pound husband. Denis thought he smelled marijuana but couldn't be sure, perhaps imagining it because of their persona or perhaps it was that cologne that smelled similar to it. He wanted to ask them if they were at Woodstock or had been in *Hair*.

Almost inevitably, the topic from the older couple went directly to Trump.

"Bernie was our last chance," Mark said, expressing the "Bernie" as if he and Bernie were old buddies.

"Oh, we'll survive," Jennifer said.

Mark shook his head glumly in the negative. "I voted for Jill Stein," he pronounced in response, nodding with a badge of pride.

Denis nodded agreeably.

"You?" he said, looking at Denis almost accusingly.

"I'm ashamed to admit, I went with the lesser of two evils thing."

"After Obama, I couldn't do that anymore."

"I understand."

Jennifer poked Denis in the side. "We should go mingle with others."

"Absolutely. Nice meeting you two."

"We love Jensen," Jennifer left behind.

After the ceremony, the crowd of a hundred or so filed into the dining area where guests claimed tables for six.

There were two open bottles of wine on the table, one red, the other white. Denis filled Jennifer's glass with the white, himself red, then guzzled it down and refilled it before others had a chance to sit and finish it off. Jennifer let hers settle.

"Go easy tonight," Jennifer warned.

"*Ja, commadante!*" He saluted with the straight-armed *heil* sign.

She laughed. "Fuck you."

The wine gone, Denis went straight to the bar. *Might as well take advantage of the free booze*, he ruminated, thinking of all the money that was purportedly in Claire's family.

Speaking of the devil, Claire arrived at their table with her parents, introduced as Robert and Vivien. Claire's mother looked a lot like Claire and not much older, fortyish, maybe fifty, but sophisticated looking and beautiful, with soulful green eyes and long hair, blond with highlights. *I'd do her*, Denis thought, even catching himself nodding and then her surreptitious look back at him, and a snide smile.

Robert looked at least twenty years older than his wife but distinguished, tall and slender, with a full head of white hair, tanned with crow's feet streaming from the periphery of his eyes and thick gorges in his neck like an aging mountain climber exposed to decades of sun.

Robert pulled up a chair next to Denis and said, "I hear you're a writer."

"I make a token effort at the craft, yes."

"I hear you do more than that."

"Have you read any of my books?"

"I don't know. What are they?"

Denis linearly enumerated the five books he had published.

"That last one doesn't sound like fiction."

"*Economy and Ecology*? No, it's my one meek effort at political science." *And last*, he thought to himself.

"What's the premise?"

And that's why, he thought. He did not want to get into a political debate now, long tiring of the subject. Trump hadn't helped.

"Well…" He paused, not knowing how to get out of this. "The premise is that capitalism has gotten us into the mess we're in."

"Mess?"

"Yes, you know, wars, climate change, exploitation of the masses and nature—the usual stuff."

"Commie stuff."

Denis sighed, and Robert laughed good-naturedly.

"You think capitalism is the cause of all this 'stuff'?"

"That's the theory of my book, yes."

"Your theory."

"Yes."

"Hardly a unique theory."

Denis took a breath.

"Well?" he insisted.

"Well, what? Did you ask something?"

"What about all the good that capitalism has rendered? Transportation, air-conditioning, iPhones, that *stuff*."

Denis saw no point in responding to what was obvious but said: "I address that in my book."

Robert nodded at him. "Is it available on Amazon?"

"Yes, of course, but I think Claire has a copy you could borrow."

"As someone who has personally benefited from your evil capitalism relatively well, I am interested in what you have to say."

The band was playing mostly fifties romantic pop, Sinatra, Tony Bennett, so on, the lead singer looking old enough to be from the era, his belly straining his tux, his receding hair and short beard snow white. But then suddenly, a young woman took the mike and began singing "Material Girl," and Denis couldn't help but think how relevant it was to the conversation he and Robert had just had.

At any rate, it offered escape from the awkward tête-à-tête, since it allowed Denis to jump up and grab the bride to dance.

12.

Denis knocked on Jim's apartment door. There was no answer. He felt the knob; it turned, and he pushed open the door. His free hand went instinctively to his nose and mouth to ward off the repulsive scent. It was then he knew.

Jim's bloated body was curled up in the fetal position in the middle of the room. Flies swarmed around his body. The room was littered with empty vodka bottles.

The situation with Melissa was getting out of hand. She was inappropriately jealous when he couldn't see her whenever she wanted to see him.

After an emotional scene at the Beveridge Place, he told her it was over.

"What?" After barraging him with a long verbal assault with offensive adjectives, suddenly she was taken by surprise. "But why?"

"Because you've come to take this relationship too seriously, and I have not."

"You *motherfucker*!" she said, resuming her verbal assault. "You make me fall in love with you; then you fucking *dump* me?"

"I didn't 'make' you do anything. You knew the situation from the start."

"No." She shook her head adamantly. "I won't stand for it."

"I'm afraid you have no choice."

"I'll tell Jennifer."

"I'd be surprised if she doesn't already know, at this point."

"Please, don't, Denis. What is it you want me to do?"

She was certainly going through the five stages of grief quickly.

"I want you to carry on with your life, as we all must do in such situations."

"I can't."

"You have to."

"You *bastard*!" she screamed.

This aroused attention around the bar, and he stood. As he was walking to the door, he felt something slam against his back. Turning around, he saw an empty schooner circling the floor like a plumb. The room had turned silent, staring at him.

He glared at Melissa one last time and then left.

One day walking in the Market, he encountered a palm reader. Just for fun, he paid her. She took his right hand in both of hers, massaged it a moment as if to draw out something meaningful, turned it over, and peered down. She gasped and looked up at him.

"What? Am I going to die?"

"You are doomed to always have three women in your life."

"Oh no." He laughed.

"Yes, see? Following your heart line here, it breaks off into three distinct lines, each of which sprouts hairline fractures, which represent heartbreaks."

They both stared some more at his palm as if there were more to read.

"Yes. It would be best for you to not have relationships at all." She nodded with conviction.

"Why?"

"Because you consistently hurt people, in your case, women. At some point, it could be fatal."

He thought back on his life, and it did seem true that since the time of his first girlfriend, there were always at least two others involved in his life in some respect, not always sexually but at least romantically to some degree. The sexual chemistry always hovered, though he hadn't always acted on it. Obviously, this was convenient with his relationship with Jennifer, since it was tolerated, even encouraged.

Now that Melissa had been excluded from this trio, he felt ready to act on another flirtation he had been having for some time in his writers group.

Her name was Dana. She wrote mysteries and was much more financially successful than he, and very popular nationally. Though the sexual tension had hovered since the start, they were both married, so there was that.

She had a long, Egyptian neck, long ,black hair, and neat, black eyes. Her skin was porcelain white, as if she avoided the sun like the plague. She had small breasts and wide hips that filled her seat engagingly. He stared at her now, as she held her glass of white wine, and she stared right back at him.

They had nothing in common. He didn't care for mysteries; she didn't care for literary fiction. The subject at hand at the moment was Knausgaard, a current literary phenom who fascinated Denis but of whom it was obvious Dana couldn't care less. He dropped it.

She was apolitical. She liked animated films; he loathed them. Nevertheless, the sexual aura hovered, and this time when the meeting broke up, he asked her out for a drink.

"We can go to my place," she said, which disappointed him, since he assumed it meant he was to meet her husband.

To add to their shared nothing in common, she lived in one of those modern boxes that took up most of a lot, three stories, hardy board siding, huge windows.

Inside was spacious, minimalist, these huge windows without shades, as if to invite in the world.

What there wasn't any sign of was a husband, only a golden retriever that greeted him at the door with savage swings of his tail, beating the shit out of himself.

"Where's the husband?" he said, leaning over and petting the dog.

"We've separated," she said, holding a glass of white wine in one hand and handing him a beer with the other.

"I see."

"But you, on the other hand, are still attached." She shrugged indifferently.

"I am."

He wanted to tell her that he had an open marriage but thought it inappropriate to act eagerly at this point. He had never been aggressive when it came to the art of seduction, allowing it to happen on its own volition, which it would if it were meant to be.

She wasn't beautiful, or even particularly well-built, in fact rather hefty, but was simply one of those rare individuals who emanated a sensual aura regardless of physical attraction.

They finished their beverages, and onward to bed.

She had a scent, emanating astonishingly from all three layers of epidermis. There was no cologne, just a smell that was intoxicating.

They were of an age that required no experimentation. She guided his hand. She came, and then he entered her from behind, a position he had been fantasizing about in regard to her for ages, that huge broad ass staring up at him as he battered away, grappling her hip bones as she displayed her erotic backside true to form.

Before he left, she informed him that he was not her only lover, implying, of course, that he needed to know this if she was to be his lover at all.

"Is that why you're separated?"

"In part."

After Melissa, this was—needless to say—ideal.

Over the following weeks, their assignations were by appointment, whenever convenient for each other. They never talked about what each was writing. They never talked politics. She never inquired about his wife, other lovers, or his life apart from her at all. They had a drink or two, went to bed; he left. It was a situation beyond ideology, philosophy, or morality, separate from their other lovers. They maintained a veil over their other lives. Sometimes there were clues, an obviously man's leather toilet bag left behind, extra toothbrushes, two half-empty wine glasses (one with lipstick), etc., but other than that, it was all kept in the dark from him.

Imbued in this enchantment of a new infatuation, he had been ignoring the third member of the trifecta. He had not been responding to Pam's texts, and then when her voice mails became frantic, he finally gave her a call.

"I was wondering if it was over between us," she answered.

"After all this time? Don't be silly."

"Well, then, get your fucking ass over here!"

"Remember what happened last time I went over."

"Oh, don't be such a wuss. That was a one-in-a-million-time thing. For it to happen again would be like lightning striking the same place one million times."

Anyway, the thought of getting caught was part of the eroticism of their affair. It was almost as if she was tempting Murphy's Law; if something could happen it would.

When Denis arrived, he realized how long it had been since he had seen her: she had let her natural color grow out, which to his surprise was salt-and-pepper. He wasn't sure he liked it since it seemed to make her face paler and naturally older. He didn't say anything, but it made him think, *All of us are all of a sudden "middle-aged,"* which kinda sucked.

After making love, he lay in bed gathering his senses and listening to her routine complaints about her husband.

"Do you have any beer?"

"You know where the refrigerator is."

He rose to fetch one. He hadn't any clothes on as he went by the window that looked out over at her neighbor's house and was reminded of what happened there last time.

Back in bed, he told her that her neighbor had seen him squeeze through the window naked.

She gasped. "Really?"

"Yes." He laughed.

"Why didn't you tell me?"

"I guess I forgot. She didn't say anything?"

"No, why would she?"

"Aren't you worried she'll tell Donald?"

"No, she gossips to me about her lover all the time."

"Jesus." He laughed. "You women."

"You *men*."

"Hadn't you already told her about me?"

"No. Only the very closest of my friends know about you."

"And how many is that?"

"Only three."

He laughed.

"I trust them implicitly."

"Now four."

"Yes, now I have something to gossip to her about."

"I'd be surprised she hasn't already seen my comings and goings."

"We should invite her over."

"Fine with me."

His lovemaking with Pam bordered on the sadomasochist arena, lots of profane assaults, calling each other the most obscene names possible, leaving red marks on buttocks, so on, short of *Fifty Shades of Grey*, but nevertheless they seemed to be excited by that degree of pain and naughtiness. Being unfaithful to their spouses was all part of it. Talk of a third party was right in there in the realm of fantasy possibilities.

Now on his third beer, he saw the day outside was turning darker, and he knew it was getting close to the time to go. He observed her in the shading light, and it made the outline of her face look near perfect, perfect chin, perfect nose, her skin showing a munificent glow, her full breasts resting contentedly on her breastbone. She looked over at him and saw what he was hinting at. She smiled.

"You'd better go."

"I know."

But then she turned on all fours and put his penis into her mouth.

13.

At the Beveridge Place, a new figure he hadn't noticed before had seemed to join the salon. What brought this man to his attention was that he could have been a younger version of himself. What was further troubling was that he thought the younger man was better looking than himself. He was about an inch taller than Denis, a height that Denis may have once occupied, since he knew he had shrunk half an inch or so. The man had the same dishwater-blond hair, though not as long, and they had similar physiques, though the younger version of himself looked more muscular, as if he lifted weights rather than ran. No one else seemed to recognize this similarity, far as he could tell, so perhaps it wasn't so at all. But Denis thought that they could have been brothers.

At this time, the young man was standing in line at the bar, and Denis went to purchase two more beers for himself and Jennifer.

The man suddenly turned to him and introduced himself, as if it had been planned beforehand: "Owen."

"Denis." They shook hands. "I haven't seen you in here before," he lied.

"Yes, I've just moved into the neighborhood, into one of those lofts along California Avenue a few blocks from here."

"How's that working out?" He sincerely was interested in how anyone could live in one of those tiny spaces.

"It's fine. I don't spend much time there. I bike to the gym and take the bus to work."

"You don't own a car?"

"No. Have no need for one."

"Where do you work?"

"Amazon."

Of course, you do, he thought but didn't ask him what he did there; he could have either been a low-paid warehouse person or a high-paid techie. Something told him it was the latter.

"What do you do?" Owen asked.

"I'm a writer."

"Oh? Do you make a living doing that?"

"I get by," he said, without elaborating.

"What do you write?"

"Literary fiction, essays."

"Ah! I write too."

"Have you been published?"

"Not yet. But I have a short story that's been accepted by *The New Yorker*."

Denis's eyes widened. "*The New Yorker*! That's impressive."

Owen shrugged. "We'll see. What's your last name?"

Denis told him.

Owen nodded. "Yes, I've heard of you. I confess I've never read any of your books, however. I will have to purchase one."

Owen paid for his beer and said, "Nice meeting you."

"You too."

He watched as Owen sat at a table with three women about Owen's age.

He took his two beers back to Jennifer.

"Who were you talking to?" she said.

"He said his name was Owen."

"He's very good-looking," she said, making no mention of any physical similarity.

"Better looking than I am?"

"Oh, Denis," she sighed. "He's younger."

"That's not an answer."

"He's a very good-looking boy. You're a very good-looking man."

"Good comeback."

They laughed.

He looked at Owen again. Denis sensed a sudden changing of the guard. Soon he would be forty, then fifty, then a bent over old man no woman would give the time of day, other than at the most kindly looks at a sweet old man.

14.

One Saturday morning as Denis was reading the paper with his coffee, Jennifer sat down across from him. He felt an unfamiliar, eerily cold aura pass in her silent presence and looked up.

"We need to talk."

Uh-oh. Those four infamous words.

"All right."

He waited.

"I think we need to have a serious discussion about where our marriage is going."

He stared at her for another long moment. "I didn't think our marriage was going anywhere other than forward."

"You and I both know we've been living a lie."

"I hadn't thought that at all… Are you leaving me?"

"That's what we need to discuss."

"Jesus, Jennifer! Where did this come from all of a sudden!"

"I know we've had this unspoken arrangement, but I think with you it's gotten out of control."

"How so?"

"I've only had Benjamin, but it seems you are mired in women."

"Not true," he semi-lied.

"How many?"

"One," he thoroughly lied.

"Oh, Denis, that's not true. Don't lie to me."

"The absolute truth is two."

"Absolute. Since we've been married, I've been with only one other man. How many women have you been with?"

He didn't answer.

"Do you even know?"

"Of course I do." In truth, he would have to think a bit.

"Then how many?"

"Three or four," he confessed to.

"See? I can't go on like this. When you're gone, I fret myself to death where you are and who you're with. I can't sleep. I go to the Beveridge Place, and if you're not there, I assume you're with a woman somewhere."

"I didn't know you felt this way. What happened, Jennifer?"

"I'm not sure."

"Are you prepared to end it with Benjamin?"

"I don't know. All I know is that I can't go on with the way things are now."

"I had always assumed that we were happy with the way things were. I knew about Benjamin, and I was fine with it."

"Of course you were. It allowed you to carry on with your innumerous fucks."

"Why now all of a sudden?"

"I don't know. Maybe I'm worried about getting older and how much longer we can maintain this façade of domesticity."

"I see."

Her eyes were busting with a film of tears.

"Did something happen between you and Benjamin?"

She shook her head no but didn't really answer.

"What's really going on, Jennifer?"

"I don't know."

"Have you stopped loving me?"

"I don't know."

"Well. That's something."

"I don't know, Denis! I really don't know!" Tears began streaming down her cheeks. "Okay! I admit it! Benjamin's wife has put her foot down and demanded Benjamin end it with me!"

"So, that's it."

"Nothing's 'it.' I just don't know. That's the bottom line."

"You love him more than you love me."

"I don't know!"

"It seems obvious to me."

"I don't know if it's that or that being rejected by him has aroused my jealousy. I really don't know, Denis!"

"Maybe we should get counseling."

"I never thought I'd hear you say that."

"I never thought I'd have the need to say it."

"Maybe I just need some time to get over him."

"Or maybe he'll change his mind."

"He seems pretty adamant about it."

"Give him time."

"In the meantime, I want you to give them all up."

"You think that's fair?"

"Why isn't it?"

"Okay…suppose I do. I give them all up…which is only two, by the way."

"Only," she scoffed.

"I give them up, and Benjamin changes his mind and wants you back. Then what?"

"I don't know."

"There's a lot here you don't know."

They sat sipping their coffee reflectively for a while. The whir of the refrigerator's fan buzzed in his ears. It was all about Benjamin. That was the bottom line. If Benjamin hadn't ended it with her, everything would be fine. *She can't do this,* he thought. *It is selfish and unfair. Because Benjamin ended it with her doesn't give her the right to suddenly make ethical judgments on his behavior!*

He had always promised her he would never leave her for another woman. It was why he married her, for goodness sake. On the other hand, most relationships ended at some point. But they were connected. They were married. They had made that commitment. Its foundation was as firm as their house's. He wondered if Benjamin was as grief-stricken as Jennifer. Or was it that he too had the same commitment: a marriage, a home, the material component of things.

"I'm going for a run."

15.

When he was leaving Dana's, at the door, he told her that he couldn't see her for a while, that his wife was demanding that he be faithful.

She said, "Okay," as if she had been told she had to give up grapefruit. To say she was not upset was an understatement. He almost thought she welcomed the news.

Pam, however, would hear nothing of it. "No," she said, adamantly.

"It's only for a while," he assured her, "until things settle down or until she's back with her boyfriend."

"But we'll still see each other. We'll just be more careful."

"You're missing the point. The point is I want to be faithful to my wife."

Pam laughed. "You? Faithful?" She continued laughing as she pushed him out the door.

But then all of a sudden, Jennifer miraculously rose out of her depression and was happy as a lamb again. Was it because he had given up his other lovers? Were they embarking into the realm of a happy married couple, until death did they part?

No. She and Benjamin were back together. All was right in the world again.

"His wife is okay with this?"

"She doesn't know. We're seeing each other on the sly."

"You'll be caught."

"No, we're going to be careful. We won't see each other when there's any possibility of getting caught."

For some reason, Denis didn't take this news well. He had in fact sort of been looking forward to being faithful, trying some of that for a while. It also again made him wonder if Benjamin was more important to her than he was.

Summer was over, and it was October, with shorter days and dreary brown skies. He looked out at the rain, at the dripping branches and the yellowing and browning leaves curling up and falling.

Pam kept calling him, but he was delaying the call back to tell her the good news. The fact was, he had been looking forward to a break from her. He wanted a break from Jennifer too. He wanted to tell her to run off with Benjamin if she wanted to. He wanted a break from women altogether; they were wearing him down.

But it only made him depressed and sick to his stomach. He realized he was going through withdrawals. He tried to write, to run— and to stay away from the Beveridge Place. But it was no good.

One Saturday, before breakfast even, Jennifer was leaving.

"Where are you going?"

"To meet Benjamin for breakfast."

She said this so matter-of-factly, it angered him.

He called Pam.

She was glad to hear from him, but of course couldn't see him: Donald was home.

"I can't talk. Call me tomorrow morning, at ten. I'll be sure to be somewhere I can talk."

"Okay."

"I mean it. I'll be very pissed off if you don't."

"Right at ten. Not one minute later."

"Yes."

But he didn't. Her command that he call ensured that he would not. It would be a Sunday, and he wouldn't be able to get together with her anyway, because her husband would be home.

Monday morning when Jennifer had left for work, he called.

"Why didn't you call me yesterday?"

"I didn't see the point. We wouldn't have been able to see each other anyway."

"But you promised!"

"What are we, twelve? I'm sorry! I'm talking to you now, aren't I? Shall I come over?"

She paused, as if thinking about it. He felt his anger rising and was about to disconnect.

"Okay," she said, but didn't sound happy.

When he arrived, he was surprised to see her dressed.

"Aren't we going to bed?"

"I don't know."

"You don't *know*?" This was really too much.

"I want to talk for a while."

"About what?"

"Do you want some coffee?"

He sighed. "All right."

They sat at her kitchen table, and she poured coffee. It tasted awful, bitter. He didn't understand what there was to talk about. They never talked. They got together to fuck each other's brains out; that was it.

"Did you know I've been sick?"

"Sick? No. How could I? You didn't tell me."

"I had pneumonia."

"Wow. I'm sorry."

"I was in the hospital for a week."

"Are you okay?"

"Yes, I'm better now. But it would have been nice to receive a little sympathy while I was going through that."

"I'm really sorry, okay? Jennifer and I are going through some serious shit."

"What does that have to do with us?"

"She wanted us to be faithful to each other."

"Oh, bullshit."

"Why do you say that?"

"Because it's impossible for you to be faithful to anyone. If you weren't seeing me, you would be fucking someone else."

"Not true."

She gave him a look that said: *I don't believe you.* Even when he was telling the truth, no one believed him.

"But that's all over now. Jennifer is back with her lover."

"And you're back with me."

"Yes."

"And it's perfect. You're free again."

"Pam, what's wrong?"

"You can't treat me this way."

"What way!"

"Like a tool to use at your convenience."

"Jesus, Pam! We're not married, for fuck's sake!"

"In a way, we are. We have a connection that's just as special as marriage."

"This is ridiculous, Pam. I can break up with you anytime I want!"

"Oh?"

"Absolutely!"

She stood away from the table, came around, and sat in his lap. She kissed him. Pam was probably the best kisser he'd ever had. She also gave the best blowjob he'd ever had. Kisses and blow jobs, the two went hand in hand.

Then she stood up and said he had to go.

"What?"

"I want you to leave, until the next time I decide I want to see you."

"What the fuck!"

She was joyful as she led him to the door. She acted as if she had performed a coup. He would always be there for her. She would be the arbiter of their relationship, not he. It was almost as if they had been in a war and she had won.

16.

Now that Pam felt secure in their relationship, they returned to the occasional long periods of hiatus from each other without worry, since she knew she could summon him whenever she was apt, since she was in charge. Their absences from each other were of no concern to her now.

When they did see each other, however, she would overwhelm him with her affections, repeating, "I love you," relentlessly, with he in turn saying, "I love you too," automatically, like saying "Bless you," when someone sneezes.

It was raining buckets, the skies a dismal dark gray. Denis and Jennifer were at the Beveridge Place.

Owen was there with these same three women. Denis tried to discern which of these women Owen might be having a relationship with but was unable to; perhaps all three. However, he acted just as if he was there with three male friends. Maybe he was gay. Gays loved to hang with women.

Owen looked over at them, observing that they were both looking at him. He rose from his seat and ambled over. He was carrying a manila envelope. "Hello, Denis."

"Hello, Owen. This is my wife, Jennifer."

He nodded at her. She smiled back.

"I was wondering if you might take a look at this." He placed the manila envelope carefully on the table in front of him.

"What is it?"

"Some scribbling. I was interested in your opinion. Of course, if you haven't the time, I understand."

"Owen, you don't need my opinion. You've been published in *The New Yorker*, for crissakes."

"I've only had a story *accepted* by *The New Yorker*. I'll believe it when I see it in print."

"Nevertheless, your talent is obvious."

There was a pause, and Owen said, "Well, all right," and picked up the envelope.

Denis grabbed it back. "No. I'll take look at it and get back to you."

Owen smiled. "I appreciate it." He returned to his party.

Denis felt like an old English professor some young student was trying to impress.

"You've never been published in *The New Yorker*," Jennifer said.

"Thanks for reminding me."

"He's very good-looking," Jennifer said.

"Yes, you said that before."

"He kind of looks like you."

"You think?"

"Yes, he could be your son."

"Son!"

"Okay, younger brother."

"Boy, you sure know how to make a guy feel good."

In fact, Denis had recently turned forty, the advent of that ridiculous euphemism "middle-aged."

Also, Denis had been experiencing a phenomenon which he had never experienced before with any real consequence: hangovers. Of course he knew that he drank more than he should, and Jennifer had mentioned the fact more than once, but he had until now held onto the myth of the hard-drinking American writing genius, the Hemingway, Faulkner, Fitzgerald, Kerouac faction, but now began to consider that his age wasn't that far from each of these writer's demise from that very dissipation. But he had always felt too that he metabolized his drinking with his running, even jumping out of bed after a night of debauchery to run any queasiness off with a six-mile run.

No more. Long nights out now kept him in bed throughout the morning, sick to his stomach, lying in front of the TV all day, even unable to write.

17.

Denis stared at the text from Melissa in disbelief: *I'm pregnant.* He automatically was going to text back, *Who's the father?* but then realized that was dumb; she wouldn't be telling him she was pregnant if he wasn't the father, or that was, the "alleged" father.

Denis had always been careful about such things. If a woman wasn't on birth control, there had always been condoms, or coitus interruptus. Melissa had been on birth control. He realized now that she no doubt had stopped in a last-gasp attempt to entrap him. He felt anger arise from the nausea he felt in his gut. He felt about to vomit.

But he shouldn't jump the gun. After all, he wasn't sure he was the father. He would require proof!

Oh my god, what am I going to tell Jennifer?

The next thought he had naturally was whether or not she would be amenable to an abortion. It would be better for both of them, after all.

They agreed to meet at Café Ladro. When he walked in, she looked up at him instantly, looking almost childlike, her hair tied back, no makeup, rosy cheeked, and smiling happily.

He ordered a latte and sat. He had to admit, she looked almost matronly. Desire rose up in him, almost a fatherly craving for the mother of his child. He imagined himself mounting her from behind, her ass broadening and inviting, her belly and breasts swollen.

Snap out of it! he told himself. He was being ensnared in a trap, and he needed to extricate himself from this nightmare! But he couldn't help himself; he wanted to go to her house right now and fuck her brains out.

She surprised him by making no demands. She intended to have the child. His involvement in the matter was entirely up to him.

His first reaction was of relief. But then he came to his senses. Melissa was fickle. He knew she could change her mind in an instant.

He didn't know what to say. *Are you sure it's mine?* occurred to him, of course, but he knew that would only make her angry. Of course the child was his; at least, she had already made it clear that she either thought it was or was insisting it was, regardless of whether it was or not. And now, abortion had already been removed from the negotiating table.

"Are you happy?" he said.

"Yes. I've always intended to have a child. And time rushes on, after all. The fact that there is no husband is a bit problematic, but I wouldn't be the first."

Denis nodded acceptingly. "All right."

She glared back at him. "All right?"

"Yes, I'll support you in whatever way you wish."

He could see by her expression that this wasn't what she wanted to hear.

"Support me? How?"

"I'm here for you. I'll support you in any decision you make in the matter. I'll support you financially, of course, so on."

"But you won't leave Jennifer."

He sighed. "No, Melissa, I won't leave Jennifer."

It was obvious the meeting had reached its conclusion. The rosy-cheeked, desirable woman was replaced with the bitter, vindictive one—just like her.

"Well, you're going to be a father, whether you want to be or not."

He nodded.

"I don't want nor need your support. I can manage on my own."

"Let's not fight. I'm here for you, Melissa, whatever your decision. If you don't want my financial support, fine. But it's early. Let's think things through." He resisted mentioning the A-word.

With this, she seemed to relax, even smile. Outside, they kissed, hugged, and that feeling of desire rose up again. She looked into his eyes as she felt his penis harden against her pregnant belly. He tore himself away.

1 8.

His biggest worry, naturally, was how Jennifer was going to react.

Studies had shown that men who are active sexually with multiple partners had elevated testosterone levels compared to men who were in long-term monogamous relationships. The reason for this was biological. When men are competing with other men for women, it increases testosterone, and more sperm is produced. When men are no longer competing with men for women, there is less sperm produced. When men in monogamous relationships discover that their partner has been unfaithful, their testosterone level skyrockets, and they react with violence, sexual desire, or both.

Men who are in a constant competitive battle with other men for women in order to propagate the species (though men of course don't consciously think this; in fact, consciously, they are oftentimes considering how to prevent pregnancy) produce more sperm than our monogamous man, who becomes more disinterested in sex as time passes, as it does with his partner. Thus, it was no surprise to Denis that he and Jennifer were in a constant state of sexual desire, and why he felt that their arrangement was so perfect for both of them.

So, it probably shouldn't have surprised Denis that that as soon as Jennifer was apprised of the news, she immediately wanted to make love. She was in competition with Denis's pregnant lover.

Post passion, each lying flat on their back catching their breath,

Jennifer said, "Do you love her?"

"No, in fact, I had ended it with her."

"Oh? Probably a mistake, in hindsight."

"She was getting too clingy."

"She wanted you to leave me?"

"Maybe."

"So, what are you going to do?"

"I told her I would support her in whatever decision she made."

"Why did you say that?"

"What was I supposed to say?"

"Do you even know for sure the child is yours?"

"I'm supposed to doubt her?"

"No, she's supposed to provide proof that the child is yours."

"A DNA test."

"Of course, unless you plan on supporting a child that may not be yours for eighteen years."

"I see your point. But she says she's not going to obligate me financially."

"And you believe that."

"I don't know."

"So, an abortion is out of the question."

"She said she's keeping it."

"And we will be obligated to support the child for eighteen years or more, depending on the decision to go to college or not."

"She said she wouldn't hold me on that, that she would be fine on her own."

"Bullshit. There needs to be a DNA test."

19.

Jennifer and Denis went for a walk through Lincoln Park. It was a beautiful Saturday afternoon, and the park was teeming with walkers, runners, soccer players, couples with strollers.

A couple sat on a bench overlooking Puget Sound with its three islands, Vashon, Blake, and Bainbridge. The man was older, sixty-ish, the woman young. At first glance, one would assume it was a man with his daughter, but they seemed more like a quarreling couple. He was leaning forward, turning to her as if beseeching her about something important, and she sat back, head lowered without speaking.

He seemed purposeful, like a man who had reached his senior years with his best years still with him, at sixty-whatever, still with a young, beautiful woman (if this in fact was true; Denis was just ruminating), her best years ahead of her if she didn't ruin herself with this older man. He seemed to be begging her for forgiveness for something, perhaps cheating?

They followed the path that descended to the shore. Though it was warm, a strong wind came off the water, and the sound was bursting with white swells.

They hadn't been talking, and he realized that this was where he belonged, with his wife, the other women in his life extraneous, a hobby, like other men had fishing or tennis. He felt it imperative that she felt the same, though he was afraid to ask her. Benjamin was a mere distraction, he fantasized, a fleeting means of entertainment.

Jennifer was someone who could not be replaced by any other woman, the woman he had chosen to marry, the woman he went to bed with each night, till death do they part.

That night they made love, and afterward she fell instantly to sleep. He lay reading a book until his eyelids grew heavy, put the book on the nightstand, and rolled over against Jennifer, spoon style.

In the morning, Jennifer was not in bed with him, and the house had an eerie, empty feeling.

Downstairs his coffee was prepared, and under his cup was a note.

I'm spending the day with Benjamin, it said simply.

She did not elaborate, as if he didn't deserve an explanation of how she was able to spend the day with her lover on a Sunday, when normally Benjamin would be with his wife.

It angered him.

He drank his coffee and read the *New York Times*, but the words went through his head like it was a sieve.

He called Melissa.

She met him at the door with an excited smile.

They embraced like long-parted lovers. When they separated, she took his right hand and placed it on her pregnant belly, even though she was showing no sign of pregnancy that he could tell. Nevertheless, she did show some sign of swelling, in her breasts and hips, yet this weight had to be more psychological than normal, as if she couldn't wait for her body to adapt to the entombed entity.

"You've put on weight," he said.

"Of course I have, after all."

"But it's only been, what—two months?"

"Yes, but the weight gain is normal, eating for two and all that. Is it that unattractive?"

"On the contrary."

"Right answer."

They laughed. In fact, she looked somehow younger, fresher, rosy cheeked like a young woman in the peak of loveliness.

"You like being pregnant, don't you?"

"I do. I've always planned on having a child one day, though I had hoped it would be with a husband. Don't you want a child?"

"I don't think men have that same instinct."

He could tell she didn't like that answer. But in bed, all instincts were put aside other than one.

Afterward, she sat up on her elbow and pushed the hair back on his forehead. "Your hair is thinning," she said.

"What?"

"It's true. You should cut it short. Balding men look terrible with ponytails."

20.

NEIGHBORS
A short story by Owen Pfeiffer

I was sixty-five and a widower. Next door was Lillian, thirty. After we got to know each other intimately, she announced rhetorically that she was a young woman, and I was an old man. Though this statement in itself was derogatory, I don't think she meant it as such; I think she was simply pointing out the illogic of our situation. It had been a long time since I had thought of myself as a young man, despite the fact that it hadn't been so long ago.

As young people tend to do, Lillian had parties all the time. Her house seemed to have an open-door policy, people coming and going at their leisure as if it were their own house.

One time a group showed up at her house on bicycles, and Lillian rode off with them for the day, returning at the end of the day drunk.

When we were alone, either I at her house or she at mine, she told me stories, as if it were she who had a lifetime of experiences to share rather than I. She made it clear to me that she had had many lovers, and I inferred from this that I was not to consider myself special. She seemed proud of her sexual prowess, like a female Casanova, and I have to admit these stories were enthralling to me. She had even been involved in threesomes, something I had never experienced but certainly had always fantasized about, but I had never been brave enough to broach the idea with my wife. Despite Lillian's and my age difference, she was indeed more practiced than I in the art of love. But then, I had been married most of my life and had been with only six women before that and had never been unfaithful to my wife.

There had been one man Lillian had loved, but he was no good, which put her off men for some time. He was a womanizer, a gambler, and an alcoholic, she explained. The pitiful part of it was that he broke up with *her.* It broke her heart, but of course it was for the best.

"I don't believe in love," she said one day, out of the blue, as if to let me know I was to not get serious.

"You've been put off it, you mean."

"No, I mean love is an ideal, like communism, a hypothesis, with no real basis in reality."

"You're young. You need more time to meet someone."

"My 'soul mate'?" she said, mockingly. "I've met enough people in my life to know that love is not real. It's a fake emotion, transitory and illusionary. People *think* they're in love, but it's only an evolutionary purpose in order to procreate. Have you ever been in love?"

"Well, obviously not, if what you say is true."

"Have you ever *thought* you were in love? Just because I don't believe in it doesn't mean you don't."

"Twice," I said, neither of whom were my wife, but I didn't let her know that.

"That's sweet."

"You must at least care about me," I argued.

"Of course, I care about you, Robert. In a certain sense, I do love you."

"Like a pet."

She laughed. "Don't be so sensitive. We're just being philosophical here."

Her house wasn't much in the way of decoration, just a sofa and some chairs put about haphazardly for comfort. There was no TV, no books or magazines. She had a laptop on her kitchen table. She seemed to take no pride in possession, of either her home or her friends and lovers. She wasn't much for housework.

"Did you love your wife?"

"I cared for her very much."

"Of course you did, but that's not an answer."

"I came to love her."

"So, you were upset with her demise."

"Of course. What a question."

The stories about her sex life had no effect on me erotically. They were just interesting stories. Besides me, there were two other men she saw on a regular basis, one married; he lived in Dallas, and she saw him when he was in town on business. The other, she especially liked to go into detail about their lovemaking. She said he could come two or three times in an hour. I didn't particularly like hearing about this, but she didn't seem to detect that. She was just talking; she liked to talk, whether I listened or not.

"But you don't love either of them?"

"I might in a way," she said, airily, and inconclusively, contradicting herself.

"Do you have a girlfriend?" she said suddenly.

"No." I wanted to say, *Aren't you my girlfriend?*

"Why not? You're still an attractive man, Robert. I wouldn't be fucking you if you weren't. You're tall and distinguished looking. There are all sorts of lonely women your age."

I didn't tell her that I was uninterested in meeting women my age.

"I like being with you," I ventured.

She smiled affectionately. "And I like being with you. I like being with men who don't have expectations."

I attended one of Lillian's parties. There was no food, just liquor. The odor of marijuana fueled in the air. I hadn't smoked pot in decades, despite the fact that it was legal now. And the last time I had smoked it was before it had evolved to the potency it was today. I took one toke, and I was high. Then I drank a beer and was messed up. I just sat there taking it all in, sipping another beer.

Lillian seemed to be focusing in on a young man. The man didn't seem cognizant of this at first, but then he came to realize he was going to get laid. As the night wore on, people filtered out, and then there was just the three of us. Lillian and this young man observed me humorously.

"It's late, Robert. You'd better go."

"He's not driving, I hope," her young suitor said.

"No, he lives right next door. You want me to walk you home, Robert?"

I shook my head and struggled to my feet. I stumbled to the door, barely remembering finding my way to bed.

The next day Lillian came over.

"Are you feeling sad about last night?" she said.

"No," I lied.

"You needn't worry about him; he's nobody."

"Okay."

She laughed. "Let's go to bed."

We went to bed and undressed. I sat on the edge of the bed, and she got down on her knees and fellated me, as if to make up for any tactlessness of the previous evening. She was the best at it as I had ever experienced, and it was over in just a moment.

Then we got into bed and cuddled. We dozed off. When we

awakened, we began to make love. I was on top of her and didn't go in all the way, teasing her. She moaned. I stared into her eyes, but she seemed focused on a spot on the wall behind me.

"*Fuck* me," she urged. "Put it into me, goddammit, and *fuck* me."

After that, I didn't see her for several weeks. I wasn't purposely avoiding her, but I decided to not go out of my way to see her either. People came and went as usual, and when she saw me, she waved as casually as any other neighbor.

Then I went over one day when I knew she was alone. I just walked right in, as everyone always did.

She was in the kitchen, fixing something to eat. "Are you hungry?" she said, as if I'd been there all morning.

"Aren't you worried that someone might just barge in and rape you?"

"It's my ultimate fantasy," she said and laughed.

We went to bed. While I was inside of her, I said it: "I love you." She looked back at me but didn't respond. "Kiss me!" she demanded. I kissed her, hard, violently.

"Say you love me," I said, "even it it's not true."

But she wouldn't do it.

And then, we began to spend more time together, like a regular couple, shopping, going to movies and dinner, etc. I decided that she loved me regardless, that she was just being headstrong. I even began to fantasize a future together.

She told me what she liked about having sex with me was that I could go a long time. Younger men came too soon. I'm not sure how this made me feel, not particularly good. But it was true. I loved it lasting a long time, because when I came, it was usually over.

Then one day she finally admitted to me that she was in love with another man. He was married, and he wouldn't see her anymore. This was before I had come into her life.

"Then you do believe in love," I said.

"I don't think you can call that love. It's more like an obsession, a sickness."

"I'm sorry that you can't have that."

"Have what?"

"Companionship with someone you care about. I call it love; you can call it what you want."

"You miss your wife very much, don't you?" she said, as if assuming that I had loved her.

"It gets easier as time goes on."

"Nothing goes on forever. We all have to deal with life as things pass on, pets, people, lovers…"

"Aren't you the philosopher today."

I went home and stared at myself in the mirror, my hair desiccated and frazzled, fat falling from my chin that looked like an old man's butt, jowls encircling my wrinkled and shrunken mouth.

Who could possibly love that?

I thought back on watching my wife slowly die and how wretched it had been and how relieved I had been when the horror was finally over.

I decided I was not going to see Lillian anymore.

But she didn't seem to care one way or another. So, I resumed going over there, and continued to do so until she moved away, about a year later, and then I never saw her again.

21.

"I'm surprised that you wrote this story from the viewpoint of an old man."

"Why? Didn't you like it?"

"Yes, I liked it. I'm just wondering why you wrote from the first-person viewpoint of an old man, when you're young."

"I'm surprised you would even ask that, as a writer of fiction. I'm projecting."

"Yes, I understand, but why?"

Owen seemed nonplussed by this question. As for Denis, he was not being kind.

"Were you inspired by another story you read?"

"No, Denis," he said, blushing. "I made it all up."

"Of course you did. I didn't mean anything by it."

"We're all inspired by other writers we admire."

He repeated: "I didn't mean anything by it."

They paused in their discourse for a moment. They were sitting at a table at the Beveridge Place. With them at the table were Melissa, Jensen, and Yi. These three were talking to one another or just laughing, it was hard to tell.

"The character has some subjective, underlying issues," Denis said.

"Now we're getting somewhere."

"His relationship with his wife, for example. It hadn't been perfect."

"Far from it."

"And Lillian too. I inferred she was abused by her father...or some other older authority figure from her childhood."

"So, you liked it."

"I already said that, didn't I?"

"It's being published."

"Oh?" Denis was startled. "Where?"

"*The Seattle Review.*"

"Congratulations."

"Thank you."

"Where are the woman friends you are usually with?"

"Changing the subject, are we?"

They laughed, took sips of their brew.

"I have no idea," Owen answered.

"Aren't one of them your girlfriend?"

"Actually, all three."

Denis stared.

He shrugged modestly. They laughed again. "There is no one I'm serious with right now."

Denis nodded.

"Did you cut your hair?" Owen said, squinting his eyes at him. "It looks different."

"Yes, I had a ponytail. Cut it to the balls."

They laughed.

"I knew something was different."

"You look the same."

They laughed again.

The evening was getting on. Owen went to purchase another beer. I turned with my beer and watched Yi, Jensen, and Melissa exit the bar without a word to me, as if I hadn't even been there. They split up, going their separate ways, each going to their respective places.

Owen sat back down and we had another beer.

The End

CHAOS THEORY
PART 1

1.

According to Einstein, we will never be able to visit the past because time is a material essence, not a spiritual one, relevant to elements in gravity. In order to revisit the past, existence has to be a fantasy, like a Jules Verne novel. All we can theoretically do is stop time, but in order to do so, we would have to travel at the speed of light—according to the famous mathematician.

But to support this sci-fi fantasy, if we could go back in time, what would we do with it? Assassinate Hitler before he killed six million Jews? Work hard to stop the production of fossil fuels before there was global warming? Change past personal behavior of which we all at some point have regretted? Or are we all bound by fate, in that all that happens is meant to happen, preordained to be part of the historical past?

The Butterfly Effect in chaos theory suggests that a minute change in one state of nonlinear systems can have a major effect on the future. The metaphorical example coined by Edward Loronz is that of a hurricane being caused by the flapping of the wings of a distant butterfly several weeks earlier. In other words, a very small change in conditions could create a profound effect on future conditions.

To augment this fantasy, if Paul's mother had had a headache the night Paul was conceived, he would never have existed, and this would have snowballed and had a profound effect on the entire planet, according to the Butterfly Effect. If we hadn't had Galileo or Shakespeare, would there have been others to fill their shoes? According to this theory—no.

Paul ruminated on this as he stood staring dreamily out his living room at the throngs of humanity in the Wallingford District of Seattle, where he had his home, sipping a local craft beer, a Manny's. If he had chosen a different craft beer when he had been at the store, how would that affect the future?

He had met Roslyn a month ago on a night when he hadn't planned on going out at all but had changed his mind after quaffing two Elysium beers, which were of higher alcohol content than Manny's. And now all of a sudden it seemed that he and Roslyn were in a serious relationship that he was considering terminating: this relationship was an impediment to the bachelor life he so much enjoyed.

He realized how unfair he was being, not to mention cowardly. They had already declared their love for each other. Yes, they had been drinking, but still…it had been vocalized, and he couldn't go back and change that, especially considering that it was true: he was falling helplessly in love.

2.

That night Paul had a disturbing dream. He had called Roslyn at 5:00 a.m. to see if she wanted to meet him before work at a restaurant they frequented. But the next thing he knew, he was at work, and it was 11:00 a.m., as if the previous six hours had never existed. He asked a colleague what had happened, and the colleague replied that they had all been worried about him because he had been wandering around the office like a zombie, not responding to anyone.

It was then Paul realized that that he was in a dream and none of this was real. Many dream experts say that dreams are clues to one's life, that they are trying to tell us something important and we should pay attention. But to Paul, dreams made absolutely no sense, and to take them seriously was silly. He was suddenly driving to the aforementioned restaurant, and then realized that he had passed it, and now would be later than ever meeting Roslyn.

Then he was suddenly at the restaurant eating pancakes swimming in maple syrup while some woman he knew who was not Roslyn was sitting across from him in the booth. He realized then that this woman he knew intimately in this dream but not in real life who was not Roslyn was not supposed to be here. He panicked, thinking that he had to be rid of this woman before Roslyn arrived. This woman was not pretty and too thin for his liking; so, what was she doing here? He looked around the restaurant frantically for Roslyn, but she was nowhere to be seen.

Then he had to pee. He was standing over the urinal trying to pee but with bashful kidneys since this same woman he did and did not know was standing next to him with an expression of clinical curiosity watching him holding his penis trying to pee. He knew that this was just part of the dream, but he was embarrassed, nevertheless. The physical components of this woman were real, however ephemeral, and Roslyn was physically absent from it.

This was then that the dream became a nightmare.

If he did indeed love Roslyn, why did he constantly betray her? He loved her despite certain flaws he was beginning to recognize. Wasn't that love? Ironically, it was the woman in the dream who was physically more recognizable to him than Roslyn. In fact, as much as he tried, he could not put Roslyn's material features into his consciousness, as if it were Roslyn who was not real.

His tennis partner and best friend, Jared, was going through a similar dilemma with his girlfriend, Anita. They each loved their girlfriends dearly but desired other women as well. For some reason, Jared wasn't burdened with the moral guilt that Paul had and even kidded him about it. In fact, Jared and Anita were in an open relationship, which he now envied.

There are no rehearsals in life, F. Scott Fitzgerald, or someone, said. We are up on a stage cold, our mistakes entrenched in concrete, the past a mirage lost in a dream.

3.

Roslyn was out of town on a business trip, and Paul used this as an excuse to go on an expedition for an erotic engagement. When he woke in the morning with an unfamiliar woman beside him in the bed, he had to gather his thoughts and put together the events of the previous evening, and then he vaguely remembered.

There was nothing physically spectacular about this woman, not particularly attractive and too thin for his liking. He got a sudden feeling of déjà vu. When she opened her eyes, she smiled at him seductively and seemed to want to make love again.

"I need coffee," he said.

"Coffee! Yum!"

He got up to prepare coffee while she ran off to the bathroom.

They sat at his kitchen table having coffee and staring out at his sparse backyard of grass needing to be cut and overrun with weeds and not much else of interest, other than a huge Douglas fir he guessed was about one hundred feet tall.

When she left, she smiled and said: "I'll call."

He couldn't remember giving her his phone number. In fact, he couldn't even remember her name.

That afternoon, he got a call on his phone from someone named Gayle.

He answered, and when she spoke, he realized it was the woman who had spent the night. Apparently, one of them had put her into his contact list.

She invited him to her house that night for dinner. He hesitated but then said okay.

She lived close, also in the Wallingford District, and was obviously why they had met, at a convenient local bar neither had had to drive to.

They made love again that night, and in the morning over coffee, he told her that he was in a relationship.

She nodded as if she had already guessed as much. "I see."

She wasn't angry, and when he left, she even said: "If you want to hook up, just call or text."

He looked at her hesitantly and said: "All right."

He was losing control over his much-cherished bachelor life, and he was not happy about it. He had enjoyed Gayle's company and wouldn't mind seeing her now and again, but there was Roslyn.

That evening Roslyn texted from the airport that she was coming over, without asking if he wanted her to, which signaled further commitment to a relationship that he did not particular want.

A taxi dropped her off. Inside the door he watched her bend at the knees, unleashing a bulky backpack with one hand and a shoulder bag with another. She looked tired but still beautiful.

Later as they lay naked, he asked her if she was spending the night.

"Of course, silly. Why do you ask such silly questions, you silly?"

In fact, he was hoping that she would go. He wanted to be alone. He wanted to call Gayle.

He enjoyed his bachelor life and had no intention of ever marrying. But he also knew that Roslyn felt that their relationship was entombed, some kind of vague future together assured.

When he woke in the morning, she was uncovered and curled

up like a wrinkled blanket. He gently pressed against her with the vague idea of making love, but she abruptly turned away from him and mumbled: "No."

Annoyed, he got up to fix coffee, and while sitting at his kitchen table, he received a call from Jared.

"Tennis this morning?" he said.

"Roslyn's here. Let me call you back."

"Cool."

When she got up and sat down across from him, he said: "Jared and I have a tennis date this morning."

"Oh, okay."

He looked at her. "Are you staying?"

"I thought I would. Why, do you want me to go?"

"No, just letting you know."

At the tennis courts, after one set, as they were resting, Paul lamented further to his only male friend his current predicament.

"Why don't you talk to her about it?" Jared said.

"And say what?"

"That you don't want to be in a committed relationship."

"I'm afraid."

Jared laughed. "Afraid of what?"

"It's easy for you to say—you and Anita have an open relationship."

"And you're afraid to suggest that to Roslyn."

"Yes."

"Well, buddy, I don't know what else to say."

4.

A month or so passed, and he had practically forgotten about Gayle. But then one day she called with the disturbing news that she was pregnant.

"What!"

"It's true, I'm afraid."

"You're not on birth control?"

"I was, but I hadn't been having sex, so I stopped."

Naturally, Paul panicked. "And you're sure it's mine?"

"*Yes*," she said, obviously irritated. "Of course it's yours. I've been with no one else."

Because of one reckless night, he had created a catastrophe that would potentially have huge consequences on not only his life but the future: the Butterfly Effect.

He of course was not in any way prepared for this responsibility. "All right then. I'll pay for an abortion, unless you have insurance."

He realized he had again said something stupid as soon as it was said, and she immediately responded: "I'm not going to have an abortion, Paul. I intend to have this child."

He then thought of the negative effect this could have on his relationship with Roslyn: *this fucking sucked a humongous appendage.*

Of course, he couldn't be sure that the child was his, only that she said it was. He told her that she would have to prove that the pregnancy was because of him before he would accept any financial responsibility, and she disconnected.

206

Curiously, she didn't call anytime soon after that, and he wondered if it wasn't true that he was the father after all and that instead she had intended to entrap him with someone else's child.

Paul believed that his relationship with his mistress Lilyana was ideal. They saw each other only intermittently. He didn't ask whether or not she had other lovers, and she didn't ask anything of his other life, though she knew now about Roslyn. The arrangement served his needs, and hers as well, since it allowed each other romantic engagements if so desired without the emotional drama of jealousy interfering. But now, of course, Roslyn complicated this idyllic situation. When he wanted to be with Lilyana, he had to make excuses to Roslyn—in other words: lie. And that bothered him.

His unwritten rule with himself was that all sentiments in his sex life were to be avoided at all costs. He had broken that rule with Roslyn. They two were sentimentally involved, and he fretted about this at the same time he was ostensibly unable to break the attachment. The more involved they became, the more he worried about the inevitable termination.

Lilyana had been a little girl in Serbia when the United States for some inexplicable reason bombed their defenseless little country into the stone ages. Her parents had had a restaurant; that and their home were destroyed in the bombing. Her family fled to the United States under refugee status. None of them spoke English. In Seattle, her father labored at one shitty job or another. He wanted to start another restaurant, but they hadn't the money, and no bank would loan it to him without collateral. On a construction site one day, he collapsed and died of a heart attack. He was forty-eight. Her mother, Lilyana, and her brother lived on public assistance.

Lilyana took up painting and after high school, studied at the Seattle Art Institute and managed to attain some local celebrity, making a good living selling her paintings. It helped that she was extremely attractive and managed to seduce her way into galleries and exhibits. She met Paul at a one-woman show in Pioneer Square. He bought one of her paintings. After the show, they experimented with different whiskeys at various bars in Pioneer Square and ended up in her charming loft in the Soho District.

Her bed, living space, kitchen, and studio were all in one spacious room that looked out over the city of Seattle from one end and onto Elliott Bay from the other. There was one sofa, one chair, and one coffee table colorfully distressed with dried paint. There was a laptop computer on a small, unfinished pine desk. There was an old record player and a space beside it reserved for LPs, which leaned against the record player. There was a small bathroom. There was no TV.

And there were her paintings, abstract works of which Paul had no powers of delineation. He had bought her painting at the show with what he thought was an act of munificence but in fact was more in quest of getting laid by this stunning blond with remarkable breasts.

The painting hung in his living room. He never looked at it.

With Lilyana, he could maintain his vow of sex with no starry-eyed attachment. One evening at the loft, he confessed his current dilemma with Roslyn.

"Uh-oh," she said.

"What?"

"Paul—are you telling me you've gone and fallen in love?"

"No."

"You have!" She laughed teasingly.

They made love as usual, and then he left, as usual. Paul seldom spent the night with his lovers, only when he'd had too much to drink. It was another of his subliminal ways to avoid any expectation of commitment. He did not want to wake up in the morning, make embarrassing sounds in the bathroom, and sit across from someone pretending to be interested in the conversation. So, regardless of what time it was, he usually left. And with Lilyana, she wanted him to be gone anyway. It was perfect.

5.

Paul's 1920s classic Craftsman home was close enough to his work to walk every morning. He enjoyed the ritual of stopping at a familiar espresso bar on the way where he ordered a double espresso and a pastry. The baristas all knew him, and he enjoyed flirting with them while they fixed his coffee. He would wolf down the pastry, swallow the espresso in two gulps, and continue on to work.

Now he oftentimes woke with Roslyn next to him in bed or he in her bed. This was disruptive to his morning routine because since Roslyn didn't drive, it meant that either he would have to drive her to work or if he was at her house, he would have to drop her off at her work before he drove home, or oftentimes, drive from there straight to work, since he would usually be pressed for time.

They tolerated this inconvenience because they enjoyed sleeping with each other. This realization that he enjoyed sleeping with someone irked him because it was an intrusion in his personal vow to avoid romantic entanglements. The euphemism that "sleeping with someone" meant having sex with someone was a false statement. There was "having sex with someone," and there was "sleeping with someone," the latter implying some degree of commitment. He had sex with Lilyana and slept with Roslyn.

———∞∞∞———

As fate would have it, Roslyn found out about Lilyana and asked if there were others. "No," he lied.

He had in fact just finished texting Maria, a colleague at work with whom he had occasional rendezvous, usually when she could safely get away from her husband.

"Are you going to keep seeing her?" Roslyn said about Lilyana, with a genuine inquisitorial expression.

"Are you sleeping with anyone else?" he said, using this very euphemism he disdained, tossing it back at her.

"No!" she exclaimed, grimacing, as if how dare he suggest it.

"Then I guess we are talking about commitment here."

"I don't know. Are we?"

"I have to go to work. We'll talk about this tonight."

"Okay, but I want you to understand I won't have a relationship with someone who can't be faithful."

"Then I guess there is nothing more to discuss."

"Oh?"

To further complicate matters, his situation with Gayle was coming to a head, with each of their lawyers close to an agreement on child support. He felt that this was monstrously unfair, since for one, Gayle made more money than he did, and two, he had no say in the matter of whether or not he wanted to be a father.

After work that evening, he met Roslyn at a bar in Georgetown close to where she worked with some colleagues of hers who were celebrating someone's retirement. Roslyn was already tipsy when he arrived; he could tell when she introduced him to everyone in an officious manner as if Paul was a mere friend and not her lover. There were people sitting on each side of her, so he took the only seat available, across the table from her. It soon became obvious to him, and seemingly everyone else, that Roslyn and the man on her left were flirting with each other. Paul saw nothing special about this man, fiftyish, with thinning gray hair, a gray mustache, and a soft, middle-aged belly. He figured she was doing this as a retribution and so did not allow himself to be angry. She seemed to be made up more beautifully than ever tonight and imagining her with this man sexually seemed inconceivable.

However, it soon became obvious to Paul, and probably every-one else, that this man—whose name was Ed—was anticipating this flirtation would lead somewhere beyond mere flirtation, and so now Paul began to be offended.

The difference between men and women in regard to flirting— Paul decided—was that for women, it was oftentimes just meaning-less fun, while for men, the ultimate purpose was to get laid, with the oftentimes end result that men would be offended while women were left confused as to why they should be.

With a few drinks in him now, he began to be paranoid and began to take the male viewpoint in this. He decided that she and Ed had been flirting around in the office for some time now, and they were about to take it to its inevitable next step, or maybe she was planning on getting even with him because of her discovery of Lilyana, and then he began to panic, thinking that this was her way of breaking up with him.

He went to the men's room to pee, and when he came out, he saw them carrying on further with this sexual banter, whether inno-cent or not, and he left without telling her.

Hiking out to his car, he texted Lilyana, but she didn't reply, and as he passed the Soho District on the highway, he considered stop-ping in on her unannounced. But it was something she insisted he never do, so instead he decided to just go home and turn on the TV.

He was sober enough to realize that his jealousy, which was based on mere conjecture, meant that he expected her to be faithful to him while of course he had never once considered fidelity to her and realized how hypocritical that was.

———∞∞∞———

In the morning Roslyn called Paul and asked what had happened to him the previous night.

"I didn't know anyone, and you seemed to be having a fine enough time without my attendance, so I left."

"You could have said goodbye."

"I waved, but you didn't see me."

"Were you jealous? "

"Of who?"

"Ed."

"Who's Ed?"

"Anyway—we weren't able to have that talk."

"Is it necessary now?"

"Why wouldn't it be?"

"It is obvious by your behavior last night that we are both free to be with whomever we want."

"You *were* jealous."

"Not in the least."

"Ed and I are friends. There is nothing between us."

"That's a contradiction."

"You know what I mean."

"All right then."

"All right what?"

"I don't know—you tell me."

"We were going to decide whether or not we have a commitment to each other."

"Or else?"

"Or we stop seeing each other. I'm not into that free-thinking 'open relationship' shit."

"Ah…all right."

"All right what?"

He discovered himself saying that which he had no intention of ever doing: "I guess we have a commitment."

"And Lilyana?"

"And Ed?"

"Stop it. I told you we were just friends. You think I would fuck that fat old man?"

He laughed. "I'll tell him you said that."

She laughed. "Now, Lilyana—she is neither old nor fat. She is beautiful, much more beautiful than I am."

"No, she isn't. I haven't seen her for a while anyway. I hardly ever saw her to begin with. Our relationship—if you want to call it that—is casual."

There was a pause; then she said: "We have an understanding, then."

"I guess."

"You guess?"

"No, we do."

"I mean it, Paul. I won't stand for you being unfaithful to me."

"I said okay."

"I'll talk to you later."

"Bye."

6.

Paul tried. But as the months passed, Paul found himself incapable of it. It simply was not in his nature to control his passion for other women. And he could not make her understand how insignificant these erotic adventures were in regard to their relationship. To him it was no different than the time he had allotted in his life for tennis with Jared. For her to expect him to abandon a recreation that fulfilled him made absolutely no sense to him, regardless of how much she told him she would no longer tolerate it. Maybe she would no longer tolerate it, but regardless, he simply could not restrain himself.

And she tried to understand this viewpoint. She even told Paul that she understood that this proclivity for womanizing did not come from some crude, ignorant display of virility. He was a cultured and intelligent man, she told him, nowhere near vulgar or without conscience. But how could *he* not understand that what he was doing hurt her so much?

And he had to admit, this nearly oblivious allure for other women didn't prevent him from feeling guilty about it afterward. And a lot of the reason he was with a particular woman was alcohol related; in other words, he hardly knew what he was doing. When he didn't drink, he didn't womanize. Only with Lilyana was he able to spend quality time without alcohol. And Lilyana was not jealous of Roslyn; that was what made it so perfect. She had other lovers as well, and in this sense the relationship functioned well for each other. But he had fallen in love with Roslyn, and this refuted his idyllic bachelor life.

And then Lilyana too became annoyed by his sudden need to leave the instant after they had made love. In this respect, an argument could be made that she was jealous of his relationship with Roslyn, despite the fact that she and Roslyn had become friends.

Roslyn knew that Paul had continued to see Lilyana, and so she had decided to establish a friendship with Lilyana to try and understand Paul's need for her. This didn't take long; in addition to being beautiful, Roslyn came to like her personally, even love her a bit. Oftentimes they kissed, and Roslyn would feel uncomfortable with it. She found herself staring into Lilyana's glassy, gray eyes, mesmerized, as if she were staring at two rounded stones at the bottom of a rushing, shallow river.

It made no sense for them to keep separate places, and since Paul owned his home (or that is, owned a mortgage on his home) and Roslyn rented, it was decided that she move in with him. The only inconvenience to this logical arrangement was that it took twice as long for Roslyn to get to work, since she had to transfer on the metro bus twice. Sometimes if she got up too late, Paul would drive her to work since, unlike Roslyn, he didn't work on a rigid time schedule and pretty much made his own hours, but it still annoyed him that he had to go out of his way.

It irked him too that there never seemed to be enough money, even after they had begun to save money living together. It didn't help that Paul now had to start paying $1,500 a month child support, along with being saddled with a $5,000 lawyer tab to add to the monthly budget, though he didn't tell Roslyn about these added expenses.

Roslyn had a modest income as well, and even though Paul had the impressive title Director of Housing Operations, it was still a nonprofit organization, the benefits great but a salary that was relatively ordinary. Roslyn pointed out to him that they were billionaires compared to what some people made—the homeless for example, a segment of society he and his company supposedly worked so tirelessly to represent—and as such, it was ironic that he complained about his own salary. If that was his attitude, she said, why not get a job in the private sector? It was a point that he could hardly argue.

After all, they both considered themselves "progressives," whatever that meant. In the last presidential election, Roslyn had voted for Hillary, but Paul had made a vow in 2012 to quit voting for the perennial "lesser to two evils" and voted for Jill Stein then and again in 2016. And in 2020, if another neoliberal was nominated, such as Joe Biden, he probably would vote Green again or some other candidate closer to his own political philosophy.

Every night on the evening news, there were reports of extreme weather all over the country, and though the established media failed to comment on its obvious cause, all over the world there was this same extreme phenomena, droughts here, flooding there, tornadoes and hurricanes everywhere, mass migrations of desperate people. Go ahead and say it, Anderson Cooper: it's called "climate change."

It had been recently reported that Canada had the fastest-rising temperatures of any country. The ice caps were melting at a rate even the climate scientists hadn't predicted. Global warming (along with, of course, nuclear proliferation) was the greatest threat that civilization had ever faced, and the world's political power structure seemed unwilling, or incapable, of dealing with it. He had recently read a political science book by a local author, called *Economy and Ecology: How Capitalism Has Brought Us to the Brink.* In this book, the suthor blamed nearly every problem we had in today's world on an economical principle based on free enterprise and said that dealing with the heating of the planet wasn't going to happen as long as we kept going along this path of constant economic growth on a planet with finite resources. Paul agreed absolutely.

To compound his financial worries, his extracurricular sexual life was curtailed considerably with the new living arrangements. But he still found time to visit Lilyana, usually after work.

One evening she opened the door naked.

"How did you know it wasn't UPS?" he kidded.

"I thought it was!" she replied brightly.

He laughed, stepped inside, pausing a moment to admire her taut, beautiful body, then quickly undressed. After they made love, he left almost as quickly as he had arrived, which again irked her.

Paul couldn't seem to make either of his lovers understand that he loved each in separate ways but equal in his affections. He could detect hints of agitation from each of them, and he didn't know how to allay this discomfort.

His love for Roslyn was unprecedented, like some new affliction he'd never experienced before. It wore at him, like a virus one can't seem to shake, constantly having to reassure her of his devotion to her.

One day at work he left to go get some lunch somewhere. He was depressed thinking about this and also about his persistent money problems.

After he ate, he went for a stroll along Northeast Forty-Fifth Street, observing all the beautiful women who returned his stare with equal attention, and to add to his woes, he became nostalgic for his previous freedom, the bachelor life that had allowed him to follow his cock like the guide of a GPS. Now he had tight shackles tugging at his balls. It wasn't Roslyn's fault—he knew that; he could break off the shackles at any time.

But in truth, he couldn't. He couldn't live without her. It was baffling. Was he really in love?

7.

Roslyn told Paul about a colleague of hers in whom she had once been interested before she met him. She admitted to Paul that she most likely would be with him now had he returned her more-than-obvious interest in him, but he at first had hesitated and then, after they had made love, quickly ended it.

Paul thought about the circumstances of this, that had she taken up with the colleague, how different their lives would be right now, and for everyone around them. One little turn of ambivalence on the part of the colleague had dramatically affected all their lives, and right now she asleep in bed beside him rather than with the colleague, and he rather than alone (or with another woman) had her in bed beside him.

One day Roslyn mentioned how beautiful her parents had been in their youth, and now, her father sixty-two and her mother sixty, they were not the least bit physically attractive.

"So?" he said.

"Sixty-two is not old."

"Old enough, apparently."

"It's just how cruel life is."

"Yes. Oscar Wilde said something about that and wrote a novel about it."

"*The Portrait of Dorian Gray.* Yes, I know. I do read books, you know."

Then why haven't I seen you reading one? he thought.

"Do you realize how close we are to being like my parents, once young and beautiful and then suddenly middle-aged and dowdy?"

"I have noticed you spend an inordinate amount of time staring into the mirror as if expecting someone different to reflect back."

"Yes—already the wrinkles have begun."

"You have nothing to worry about. You're still beautiful."

"That's easy for you to say—you're a man. Wrinkles mean nothing to men—in fact, men are better looking with some wrinkles because it gives them 'character.' It means they are no longer boys. There is no character with wrinkles on women. Men want women to stay girls forever."

"Are your parents happy?"

"They seem to be. I know, however, my mother hates getting old."

"Well, then they have their happiness with each other to compensate for their loss of beauty."

"Why? Aren't you happy now?"

Paul didn't know how to answer this. Happiness had never been a condition he had ever considered in regard to himself. "I'm happy with you."

"Right answer." She smiled.

But Paul had to think whether or not that was even true.

Paul and Roslyn had taken to running around Green Lake every evening after work, about a three-mile run. The lake was green because of algae in the lake and the reflections off surrounding evergreens. This additional habit to their daily routine seemed to confirm them as a couple, an "item," went the saying. Paul detected that it seemed to give Roslyn a warm feeling of security. However, as they passed other pretty women running in the opposite direction, it occurred to Paul that he could just as likely be with any of them as

Roslyn. Or was his relationship meant to be—"in the stars," as they said. Or was it simply a matter of circumstance and coincidence? He watched as men ogled Roslyn; she didn't seem to notice.

Despite the fact that Paul had continued to be unfaithful, Roslyn remained convinced that eventually she would have to put her foot down on the issue if they were to remain a couple. She was resolute about this.

Her father had been a profligate womanizer, and it had been a major issue in their marriage, but her mother had stayed with him regardless until age had had its inevitable consequence, both in looks and presumably desire, and the womanizing came to a halt, according to her mother, at any rate. Her mother had simply waited until he had got it out of his system. She was determined to not be like her mother.

She was over at Lilyana's one day without Paul, and Lilyana said she wanted Roslyn to pose for her.

"Really?"

"Yes. The painting will be a present for Paul."

"How long will it take, you think?"

"We don't have to do it all at once. In fact, I can photograph you and paint it from that."

"All right, then."

"Take off your clothes."

"What!"

"It will be a nude. Don't you think Paul would like that?"

"I think he may wonder."

"About what?"

"Why I would pose for you naked."

"Because that's what painters do."

Roslyn laughed. "We'd better have a drink first then."

Lilyana laughed and hopped to her feet to fetch a bottle of Chianti.

They drank the bottle down and were giddy. Roslyn undressed, and Lilyana took a series of photographs of Roslyn in various positions and poses.

After she finished, Roslyn dressed, and they inhaled another bottle of Chianti, and then Lilyana kissed Roslyn. This time the kiss lingered longer than usual, and as such, a bit unnervingly.

Roslyn was shocked, not so much from the kiss but by how much she had enjoyed it. She had kissed girlfriends in adolescence, but that had not been sexual, she didn't think; they were experimenting, learning how to kiss properly.

"Are you bi?" she asked Lilyana.

"No," she said reflectively. "At least, I don't think so. I don't put labels on that kind of thing. If it feels good, I do it without intellectualizing about it too much. It was just a kiss, after all."

"Yes. It was nice."

"Let's not dwell on it beyond that."

"I hate to admit this, but I'm finding myself not quite as jealous as I should be in regard to your relationship with Paul."

"I'm glad to hear that."

"For some reason I don't find you a threat."

"I'm not...Paul's and my relationship is based solely on the physical. He and I could never have what you have with Paul."

"Which is?"

"Love."

Roslyn stared reflectively at Lilyana for a moment, unsure if she believed that Lilyanna didn't love Paul and that Paul didn't love Lilyana in some abstract way. It was inconceivable to her that two people could have sex and that it not be more than just the carnal.

They went over the photographs, trying to decide which one to use for the portrait.

"I don't have a bad body," Roslyn reflected.

"Why are you surprised?"

"I guess because I've never been confident with my body."

"You should be. You should be delirious."

They laughed, drank more wine, and kissed intimately again, longer this time, each touching the other. Lilyana moved the tips of her fingers softly along Roslyn's clothed back. Roslyn felt something arousing by the kiss and the touch, but not sexual—she didn't think.

Nevertheless, Lilyana stood and removed her top.

"Stop," Roslyn said.

"Why?"

"I'm not sure what this means."

"Nor do I. I'm just following my instincts. How about with Paul present? I'm sure he wouldn't mind."

They laughed like schoolgirls. Then Lilyana resumed undressing.

8.

When Roslyn was a college student working part-time as a server in a Greek restaurant, each evening the restaurant owner would ask when she was going to go out with him. She repeatedly said, "Never," and laughed. It became a little joke between them. Neither was offended. She liked him. He was charming, very handsome, not tall, about thirty-five, with thick, curly hair and a sexy swatch of gray across his forehead. He had a bit of a paunch, but it seemed almost endearing on him. But he was married and had a reputation of sleeping with the help. The one-sentence interrogation and answer carried on unremittingly, and then one day she agreed to sleep with him. He didn't act surprised, as if he knew his persistence would inevitably have its way.

So, they had sex, and the sex was good; in fact, it was the first time a man had succeeded in bringing her to orgasm. But he never asked her out again. She realized that she had been considered a conquest, nothing more.

She thought about the restaurant owner's wife, how since Roslyn was detached emotionally from the poor woman, it had no negative mindset toward her boss. Despite that, she felt guilty for being unfaithful to her gender. She realized that she had now become that wife, not married, however, living with a man who had other women besides her.

Lilyana had another regular lover besides Paul, who was married with children. It didn't take a psychologist to understand that Lilyana took lovers who were attached to others to avoid commitment. Neither of her lovers knew about the other, and one of her strict rules was that neither called on her unexpectedly. Her other lover had done this once, and she refused to answer the door, even though she was alone and not expecting anyone.

He had then called her on his phone while standing outside her door, and she answered.

"Where are you?"

"At home."

"What? Then why aren't you answering the door?"

"Because you hadn't called first to see if I was available."

"Oh, fuck," he said, impatiently. "Well? Are you available?"

"Yes."

"Well, then, open the fucking door!"

This other lover's name was Peter. Peter and Paul; it had a fluky alliterative ring to it. He was a professor of English literature at the University of Washington. He was tall, perhaps an inch or so taller than Paul, and very popular with his students, she had surmised. He lived in West Seattle on the water along Alki Beach.

Peter was in love with Lilyana and told her so repeatedly, without reciprocation from Lilyana of the sentiment, which exasperated Peter. She did love Peter, as she did likewise Paul, but she was not *in* love with either because she simply refused to submit to that sentiment. She was dogged in her pursuit of independence and knew she would grow old and unhappy, since anyway, she was certainly unhappy now and preferred being so alone.

Peter, for his part, knew that falling in love with someone besides his wife was a mistake because he had been through this too many times before to not know that the only eventuality of this would be heartbreak. Peter was a romantic.

One day Peter called and asked if he could come over. She was working but said all right. When he entered, she put down her paint brush (she in fact was painting the portrait of Roslyn) and went for a bottle of red wine for them to sip. When she came out with the wine, he was looking at the unfinished painting but made no comment. She realized the karmic coincidence to all this: Lilyana, Peter, Roslyn, and Paul.

They clinked glasses and swallowed their wine all at once. They laughed, and she refilled their glasses. This, of course, was their usual pretext for love, and they both were excited.

But Peter was not content and in fact obviously insecure. His intention with his lovers was that they fall in love with him, not the reverse, and it angered him that Lilyana refused to submit to this sentiment.

Peter carried around a deep, emotional scar. He had suffered from depression his whole life, and it had not helped with therapy, even with antidepressants. He had not gone to kindergarten because they didn't have kindergarten in Anchorage, Alaska, where he lived with his family at the time. On his first day of first grade in Seattle, an older neighbor girl had accompanied him. However, after school was over, she wasn't there to accompany him home. He waited until there was no one else coming out of the school. He looked back and forth onto the street, and it was dead still. He started home.

On the way a man approached him suddenly and said: "Hey, kid, come 'ere."

He sensed it necessary that he follow this man into a garage, where the man shut the door behind him, and what happened after that was a blank.

Afterward he suffered from stomach ailments, diarrhea, and insufferable headaches. He suffered academically. One day he stood up in class and walked home to go to bed because his sinus headache was more than he could bear while in class.

For a period, he was taken from class daily to talk to someone. She was a therapist, but of course he did not know this when he was six. He liked her, in fact, had a crush on her and didn't like that the hour with her went by so quickly.

The following months were a blank as well. On the first day of second grade, he stood outside the door not wanting to be late and also to be able to have his choice of seats, which would preferably be in the back. But then suddenly the class was full, and he was still standing outside the door. These holes in his consciousness would occur throughout his life. He never told any of his therapists about his experience with the man when he was six years old, simply because he did not relate whatever had happened to his depression.

Sitting here now with Lilyana, she fixed Peter with an intense stare and said: "You went away again."

"Sorry."

Her stare confounded him. Was it just physical passion that bore into him with those mysterious gray eyes? Or was she angry with him about something? It in fact was neither. It was simply interrogative. She was wondering where he went when he blanked out. But he did not know himself, so he could not say.

But he intuited something else. He felt it was a turning point in their affair.

"Is there someone else?" Peter said.

"Peter, I've told you before: it's none of your business."

He sighed. The exasperating topic was draining for both of them, and neither of them could understand why he kept pursuing it.

They swallowed their wine and got undressed.

When Peter was alone, he would imagine Lilyana with another man and get an erection. He knew that this was consistent with the Madonna/whore dichotomy, his mistress of course his whore and his wife, Caitlyn, the Madonna. He fantasized watching Lilyana being fucked by another man, and this fantasy was compounded by the fact that she did have sex with another man, or perhaps even other men besides himself. In other words, he compartmentalized his life with his wife and mistress, but nevertheless, the love he felt for each was constant.

Lilyana, for her part, did not share these sentiments of love with him, or Paul.

After they made love, Peter got dressed and hurriedly dressed as usual, to avoid confrontation with his wife. She was irked that it was beginning to bother her that her two steady lovers needed to get away so quickly after sex.

She stood before her full-length mirror naked and tried to cognize herself from an objective viewpoint. She knew that her situation was not unusual. In fact, she occasionally had one-time encounters with other men as well, and when these men wanted to see her again, she refused. They were exhilarating to her, even though these one-nighters seldom resulted in orgasm.

The next time Peter was over, they made love with an extra energy that surprised them both, almost like a parting gift. When she came, she cried out in tears. She did not understand this sexual combination of grief and passion. Neither did Peter.

Lilyana did not consider herself a feminist, at least not in the conventional sense. She was not militant in her individual demands. Her independence was a statement in itself, a human one, not one of gender.

Sated, Peter collapsed over on his back, breathing hard. He blurted out: "God! You are a *woman*!"

She turned her head toward him, lying on her back in post-orgasmic gratification, watching him catch his breath. She tried to understand what he meant by stating the obvious. Why not say: "You are a *human*!"

"If I am a woman," she said, "what is your wife?"

He turned his head to her without answering. When he left, they hugged with an unspoken understanding that they had reached the peak of their relationship and they were now on the downward slope.

Peter left deeply in despair.

9.

Years earlier, Caitlyn had left Peter and told him she would not return until he could agree to be faithful to her. So, he agreed, and was sincere, but simply was incapable of keeping that promise, and now she seemed resigned to it. She needed Peter for the support he provided, wasn't sure if she even loved him anymore, and was even contemplating taking a lover herself, if only to see how he liked the tables turned.

Peter had been told in therapy he had issues with his mother, in the traditional Oedipal sense. Caitlyn even looked like his mother once had, with the Northern European look, and one time his mother had left his father for a time because of his father's infidelity. He hated his father because of it.

He told his therapist about Lilyana, and the therapist said he looked at Lilyana as a mother figure, despite her being twenty years younger. Peter rolled his eyes when she had said that and was thinking of discontinuing therapy. It never occurred to Peter that he might be evading harsh realities.

Peter was more focused on pleasing Lilyana than was Paul. For example, she would lie flat on her stomach, spread her legs, offering herself, his head, his nose, sucking and licking at each orifice, delirious, vertiginous, his prick about to burst. He would dine and luxuriate at her delectable leakage. It would go on for some time, Lilyana delaying it as long as possible, until she could stand it no longer, and just as she was about to arrive at the crucial moment,

Peter would lurch into her and they would orgasm together. No man had ever done anything like this before.

And Peter too was addicted to her bewitching power; she was the night bitch Lilith. Nothing could keep him from her clutches. He had tried.

And Lilyana too was bred more on betrayal than loyalty. To her, betrayal was an act of conscience, a rebellion against the staid moral code society had invented for the sake of puritanical nonsense. Lilyana loved nothing more than being herself with her art and not propped up by the puppet strings of some man, and she attempted to express this in her art.

She was fortunate to make a living at her craft. She knew many painters just as talented as she living by the skin of their teeth, having to supplement their meager incomes with jobs they hated. Unlike Caitlyn, she didn't need a man to take care of her. To be dependent on someone, especially a man, was unthinkable to her.

Peter had published two books, one a collection of short stories, the other a novel. Nevertheless, he too had to supplement his passion for writing with a job, but at least a job for which he held some interest. He was not Stephen King or James Patterson. He wrote literary fiction, and neither of his books had done well, and his agent was having trouble selling his current book to a publisher. Peter would often denigrate these popular writers who were so financially successful.

"Oh, quit whining," Lilyana said.

She had not read his books, and this irked him. Since she was a patron of the arts herself, he thought she would appreciate all the arts—not just painting, but music and writing, the latter art of which Peter lived and breathed. That, and working out with weights, helped salve his ever-looming depression.

Caitlyn couldn't understand why he couldn't be happy. He had everything most men would envy: a good career, a beautiful home, and a loving family. She couldn't seem to understand that he didn't like being depressed; he would have given his soul for some peace and contentment.

The closest Peter got to being happy was when he lay on the sofa with his eyes closed and listen to Mozart, Shubert, Beethoven, Tchaikovsky, those of the baroque era. His father had been a classical violinist, but he couldn't make a decent living at it, so he had to give it up and become a cabinetmaker, like Peter's grandfather, and the father before that. But as much as Peter adored music, he unfortunately had inherited his ear for music from his mother, who couldn't find the note to save her life. But he could listen to it and appreciate it. He loved all music, not just classical, but rock, country, jazz, and blues. He had yet to allow himself to try and appreciate rap.

Once in his office at the university he was singing along with Elton John's "Levon." A current student lover was in his office with him at the time, a girl of eighteen, who said: "Who's that?"

"Elton John."

"Why don't we just let Elton sing it?"

That's how bad his voice was.

But of course, it was literature that Peter fixated on because he was a writer himself. But when he began to pontificate on some writer or another, such as Faulkner or Fitzgerald, Lilyana would tell him he was boring her. And though no one else would say anything so blunt, he could tell when others felt the same. He knew that most of his students were sitting in his class simply for a credit.

If Paul knew about Peter, he would be surprised, since Peter was pushing sixty and looked his age, with thinning gray hair and a bit of a paunch. He was still handsome, however, with thick muscles, and the act of seduction was still innate for him, especially with his students, of whom he had bedded at least forty.

Once Lilyana had accompanied Peter to a party of academics. She could tell by the looks of his colleagues that they were envious of Peter's inexplicable fortune in this erotic department.

They were discussing politics. All of them, it seemed, tilted decidedly to the left, and the topic of Trump was off the table, his existence too absurd to merit even comment. Almost all of them seemed to prefer Bernie Sanders as a candidate for president.

"I'm concerned about his foreign policy," someone said.

"What foreign policy?" someone else said.

"Exactly," the first one said, and there was laughter.

"He doesn't mention Israel much," another said.

"Too toxic," someone new said. "He doesn't want to lose the Jewish vote."

Even Bernie Sanders was not up to the intellectual level of these people.

"And what do you do?" someone said to her, another man about sixty, who had been eyeing her from the gitgo.

She told him.

"Oh! What's your name?"

She told him.

"Do you have any paintings in galleries around town?"

She told him where.

Peter arrived with another glass of wine, putting his arm proudly around her waist, seemingly to indicate custody.

The topic moved on to climate change, and they all seemed resigned to the fact that at this late date there was nothing to be done: we were screwed, seemed the consensus.

It all bored Lilyana to no end, and she was sorry she had come and had not gone instead out with some friends her own age who knew how to party and not think about climate change. Yes, she supposed the ice caps were melting, but she was estranged from that and all other political issues. These old fuddy-duddies seemed to use politics as an item of entertainment!

And Peter was as tedious as the others. She had already heard him declare with bravado that he was a socialist, as if that was unique. He expounded on Marx, and this too bored her to tears as he went on about "surplus value" and the "petite bourgeois," of which he didn't seem to realize he belonged. He blamed capitalism for literally all the problems of the world and mentioned a book that everyone should read called *Economy and Ecology: How Capitalism Brought Us to the Brink.*

Finally, Lilyana couldn't take it anymore. One night at her loft she told him he had to stop.

"Stop what?" He looked genuinely inquisitive. He sipped at his glass of $150 scotch.

"Your incessant pontificating! Whether it's literature, politics, film, music, or art—you can't shut up for a minute! I'm serious—if you can't stop, then I'm afraid you and I will have to stop seeing each other!"

Peter was astonished. Didn't she realize it was her generation that was most affected by the current political arena? Was she really so apolitical?

"Yes, I'm apathetic," she confessed. "You know why? Because it doesn't matter. You know damn well Bernie Sanders doesn't stand a chance being nominated. You and all your intellectual friends are wasting your breath."

"As long as there are people like you, you're right. You have to at least try to make the world a better place."

"No, I don't."

"There you are: we're doomed."

"Your lecturing has such a lofty air of righteousness, as if your opinions are the only ones that matter."

That at last hit a nerve. He did not know how to defend this accusation. He got up without another word and left and did what he always did when his being was attacked: withdraw into his safe, indignant shell.

The next time he called Lilyana, she didn't answer or return his call. He then texted her, but she didn't respond to that either.

10.

Lilyana decided to have a party. She invited Paul and Roslyn and also invited Peter and his wife. She was roguishly interested in having them all meet.

"You want me to bring my wife?" Peter said, surprised that she would. "Why?"

"I want to meet her."

"Why?"

"Quit asking why; just bring her."

"Why haven't you been answering my phone calls?"

"No reason."

"No reason!"

"Don't be so possessive."

She watched his face turn pink with rage.

"Anyway," she said. "Will you come?"

"I'll see if she wants to."

"Good."

The four of them did come to her party. Lilyana was highly amused by this. Peter and Paul didn't know each other of course, and she was curious how they would interact.

Marijuana was legal now, as if that made any difference, and the sweet, pungent odor wafted through the spacious loft. Peter and Caitlyn didn't indulge, however.

"We smoked enough pot in the seventies to last a lifetime," Caitlyn explained.

Lilyana was surprised that Caitlyn looked nowhere near the age she had to be. Her face was unlined, and her thick hair was a lustrous strawberry-blond. Lilyana couldn't help but notice that her breasts were even larger than her own. They were about the same height. She was a very attractive woman; Peter was a lucky man.

She manipulated the crowd and managed to have the two applicable couples meet. They got along splendidly. Peter and Paul especially seemed to hit if off.

"How do you know Peter?" Caitlyn said.

"He was at one of my shows," she replied truthfully. *And that night we fucked our brains out*, she thought. She actually felt a twinge of competition.

"You're a wonderful painter," Caitlyn said.

"Thank you."

"I believe we have one of your paintings hanging in our living room."

"Oh?"

Peter got drunk. When someone offered him a hit off some pot, he said: "That stuff will rot your brain!"

"And that won't?" Lilyana said, nodding at his drink.

"All the great American writers drink! Hemingway! Fitzgerald! Wolfe! Algren! Poe! Anderson! It's as American as apple pie!"

"Are you comparing yourself to these writers?"

Caitlyn observed the familiar rush of anger flush Peter's cheeks. His eyes narrowed. Suggesting that he was any less than a great writer threw him into an unpredictable rage.

"I think we should go," she said.

"Yes, yes, okay," Peter said and rushed off to fix himself another drink.

"I hope you're driving," Lilyana said.

Caitlyn stared at her. "How long have you been fucking my husband?"

"I'm not!" she blurted out. The question startled her.

"Uh-huh." She promptly turned on her heels to collect her husband, Peter balancing his drink as Caitlyn dragged him to the door.

Lilyana was impressed. Caitlyn was a strong woman and had no intention of ever letting her husband go. This amused her.

Peter was a strong man as well, if only physically. Recently she had been with him downtown when two young white men were harassing an elderly black man, demanding that the older man hand over his wallet. The old man refused, and one of these young men grabbed the older man while the other grappled at his clothing, hunting for his wallet.

"*Hey!*" Peter yelled, rushing at them like a man half his age.

Two blinking punches later, the two young men were sprawled out on the wet sidewalk, groaning in pain.

"You all right?" Peter said to the elderly man.

"Yes, thank you." Peter brushed the poor man off, observing him carefully.

"Are you sure you're going to be all right?" he reiterated, as he observed the two assailants run off down the street.

"Yes, yes," he said. He almost looked irritated. "I can take care of myself!"

As he returned to Lilyana, she said: "Wow."

"Assholes," Peter said.

"You're a *man!*"

Peter looked at her ironically. She seemed to have forgotten what he had said about her one evening after making love: "You are a *woman!*"

Then he elaborated on how his father had taught him how to fight after coming home from school too many times beat up by bullies. When he was fourteen, he began to lift weights, and it became a routine he pretty much had maintained all his life.

Peter was a man's man and a lady's man. But she knew that

Peter had deep insecurities that came from somewhere. He was a published writer but unsatisfied with that. He yearned for fame as an author while at the same time seemed terrified that the world would discover that he was a fraud. He told Lilyana that his best work went unpublished while his mediocre work was accepted. It was puzzling. He was always surprised when a literary magazine published a particular story while rejecting another he thought more worthy.

At the beginning of their affair, one time in her loft when she had returned to him with their drinks, he was staring across the room in a trance.

"Peter?" He didn't answer.

She shook him, and he came out of it.

"What was that?" she said.

"What?"

"You were staring across the room like a zombie!"

"I was?" He reached for his drink, shrugging as if it was no big deal.

One night shortly after the night of the party, over at his loft, settled in with drinks, he said: "Caitlyn's demanding that I quit seeing you."

"Do you always do what your wife demands?"

"I knew I shouldn't have brought her to the party."

Lilyana now decided it was imperative that their affair carry on. It had become a duel.

"Caitlyn's extremely intuitive," Lilyana said.

Peter shrugged. "She's a woman."

There it was again, that sexist assumption of gender significance.

That night she made love to Peter with more ferocity than ever. She concentrated on what she knew he liked, using techniques she knew, from what Peter had told her, Caitlyn never applied. She wanted him to know what he would be missing. After he had climaxed, he collapsed on top of her in a heap, whining like a broken man. Peter post-coitus was helpless as a child.

But then, she stopped hearing from him.

She fell into an unusually deep melancholy. She couldn't stop thinking about the last time they had made love and was dismayed that he could give that up.

She realized that it had been a mistake to refer to him as a "man." He wasn't a man: he was a frightened child sucking at the prominent teats of a dominant wife.

She was surprised at herself for missing him like she did. It was only after he had rejected her that she realized how much she cared for him. Only in his absence did she become so obsessed with him that she barely gave Paul a thought. All she could do was ponder schemes on how to get him back. She was even considering texting him and saying that she wanted him to leave Caitlyn and move in with her. But then she realized how desperate that would appear and changed her mind.

Peter and Caitlyn had been married a long time. She knew that had to account for something.

But the obsession carried on unrelentingly. She decided to attend one of his classes at the university. She was anticipating a large hall packed tight with students and was surprised to see a small classroom, the seats only half-full.

He was standing at a podium when she walked in and took a seat. He saw her but conveyed no particular expression, pro or con.

"Why do you think second wave feminism had issues with Lawrence?" he carried on with his discourse.

There was no response from anyone, so he said: "Do you know

what I mean by 'second wave'? Anyone?"

"It's the wave that comes after the first one," a male student said.

Everyone laughed, even Peter.

There was still no response, so he went on: "If the first wave refers to the suffragists of the early twentieth century, which led to the women's right to vote, what would be the second wave?"

"Gloria Steinem," a student said.

"Yes, good, Gloria Steinem was a popular and important character in the movement. And Kate Millet, Betty Friedan, Germaine Greer, and many others who emerged in the 1960s and 1970s as symbolic of that era, analogous with the progressive antiwar and civil rights movements, which shaped a growing awareness of the rights and inequalities of women. This was called the second wave.

"Some of these women had issues with a man writing from a woman's sexual viewpoint. Kate Millet argued in her book *Sexual Politics* that Lawrence wrote about men's genitalia as a token of power over women, contending that Lawrence presented men as dominant and women as submissive and absent of individual thought.

"However, others, such as Erica Jong, held no such resentment and admired Lawrence and other sexually explicit authors such as Henry Miller for their literary stylishness. I tend to agree. There is a lot in Lawrence's novels that empathize with women's sexuality. For example, in one scene in *Lady Chatterley's Lover*, Constance is able to have an orgasm with Mallory only after he has become flaccid, and he takes offense that she is unable to do so while he is erect. Here is the male who if flawed, humble, embittered, not understanding that sexuality is an individual matter, not a dominant one.

"In *Women in Love*, Gudrun is an extremely dynamic personality who falls in love with Gerald but soon becomes bored with his masculine posturing, which is in fact indicative of deep-rooted insecurities, and she drives him into submission. While it is perhaps true that one can criticize Lawrence for pretending to understand women from the viewpoint of a male, all writers of fiction pretend, don't they? That's what being a writer of fiction is, pretending and creating one's own characters, whether from the viewpoint of a man or from the viewpoint of a woman. A male writer of fiction should be able to write from the viewpoint of a female, and vice versa, the only measures that of talent."

———— ✳ ————

After class, Peter and Lilyana went for coffee.

"I'm surprised to see you here," Peter said.

"Are you? You didn't act surprised. You looked exactly as if you were expecting me, as if I were one of your students."

He laughed. "Maybe not so much surprised as curious. Why did you come?"

"Just wanted to sit in on one of your classes."

"Uh-huh."

"And I'm not surprised that you would choose D. H. Lawrence as a topic."

"The class has been assigned to write a critique of *Women in Love*."

"Why not *Lady Chatterley's Lover*?"

"Because *Women in Love* is the superior novel, and more complex, especially from these viewpoints of gender. *Chatterley* is more of a spoof, a spit in the eye to the staid mores of the time."

"Will you come see me tonight?"

"Miss me?"

"I miss your cock."

He shook his head. "You are some woman, I'll grant you that."

"Will you come or not?"

"I guess it's not over, is it?"

It will be over on my terms, she thought and leaned across the table for his lips.

11.

One night Roslyn arrived home late after going to a pub with friends, and Paul was already in bed. She washed her face and hands and brushed her teeth as always before going to bed and joined Paul under the sheets, anxious to cuddle up to him. But as soon as she did, she realized that Paul had not partaken in this pre-bed hygiene ritual. His breath stank of stale alcohol, and the odor of sex emanated from his body. She grabbed his right hand and brought it to her nose, detecting the pungent odor of another woman's unwashed vagina.

She got up to sleep in the guest bedroom. She would not be able to sleep with that nauseous odor penetrating her senses.

In the morning, Paul was up before her, as usual preparing the coffee for both of them. She had always been charmed by this trifling act of domesticity. But this morning she couldn't get the odor out of her mind, intact in her olfactory system as if she could still smell it. She thought she had gotten used to his other women but realized now that she could no longer bear it. Lilyana was one thing, but one-night stands were no longer tolerable, especially with women whose hygiene was questionable.

"You should have washed before you went to bed last night," she said as he put down her coffee on the kitchen table.

"What?"

"I could smell your whore on you."

Paul reflexively put his right fingers to his mouth then abruptly put his hand behind his back as if to hide it.

———⚬⚬⚬⚬———

Roslyn's father had been a compulsive womanizer, and her mother had tolerated it. Roslyn had always wondered why she did, but since her mother was a homemaker with no career to back her up, perhaps she was terrified about having to make it on her own. Regardless, she remembered when she was twelve years of age a man coming to their home to talk to her mother. They had coffee and were talking respectfully, and then this man calmly told her mother that if her father ever came near his wife again, he would kill him. Then he left.

That night she couldn't sleep over the yelling and screaming of her parents.

Then she was startled by a commotion emanating from her parents' bedroom and realized they were having sex. She listened to the voluminous moans of her mother, almost as if his unfaithfulness was some kind of twisted foreplay.

In the morning, things seemed normal, as if her parents had made up, as if the sex fixed everything.

They never divorced, and her father continued to womanize until age and presumably desire caught up with him.

Now she wondered if she had become her mother and had fallen in love with a man who was just like her father. Paul even looked a bit like her father. This Freudian possibility tore at her conscience. Even his relationship with Lilyana now tormented her.

Later, looking at her naked body in the full-length mirror in the bedroom, she wondered why Paul couldn't be satisfied with it. She had a good body, her normal-size breasts perky, her stomach flat, and her bottom two taut mounds free of cellulite. She couldn't seem to grasp this point that Paul had tried unsuccessfully to implant in her stubborn consciousness, that it had nothing to do with her or her beautiful body, that he loved her while at the same time craved other women. She knew that some if not all men were like that, whether they acted on the compulsion or not, and Paul acted on it apparently because he could.

As she continued to gaze at her body, she knew that all too soon the contours of her youthful body would change with the condemning effect of time, at an ever-accelerating rate. In a sudden blur, her breasts would sag and her perfect behind would be afflicted with pockets of cellulite. But Paul too would soon no longer be handsome. She noticed already his hair showing signs of receding. Would he pursue younger women, as many older men did? Was this the curse that women lived under?

And then suddenly, this perfect body reflected before her began to disgust her, since she realized it was nothing more than a convenient receptacle for men's carnal desires. There was no love behind the physical craving. She was like a bitch in heat where pheromones attracted all the male mongrels in the neighborhood. When she was out on the streets, men sniffed her out like hounds. The disgusting aroma on Paul's fingers was a siren's call. The whore's smelly cunt summoned Paul like the nectar that summoned butterflies and bees.

If she stayed with Paul, it would not be as his soul mate but as just another body there for his convenience. She decided right then and there that she would no longer be just another docile woman there to satisfy Paul's needs as her mother had her father's.

She would be like him.

PART 2

1.

Roslyn and Lilyana were more friends than lovers. They enjoyed the feel of each other's smooth flesh, but they enjoyed each other's company from an aesthetic and philosophical viewpoint even more. They sipped wine and talked. They went to restaurants to dine and converse. The relationship that women friends have is in some ways more challenging than their romantic relationships, more intimate and confidential. They chose not to share this particular intimacy with Paul, preferring the company of just each other. Paul was happy about the friendship and thought that was all it was. In some ways, Lilyana and Roslyn grew to love each other as much as they loved Paul.

And at work Roslyn allowed a flirtation with a coworker to work its normal course. Women are inclined to look on flirting as innocent fun, while men as a rule perceive it as a precursor to sex. They are both wrong. Flirting is a sexual communication but not a guarantee of sexual congress.

Roslyn was an attractive woman and much more attractive than she realized. She was always surprised when men came on to her, as if she were undeserving of the attention. She was especially surprised when attractive men did this, men such as Paul. Paul had brooding good looks with sexy streaks of gray just beginning in his coal-black hair and a body hardened with weights he had in his basement. Paul's unleashed her own previously veiled inhibitions, and she allowed her flirtation with Jesse to follow whatever destiny it prescribed. Jesse was the exact opposite of Paul: jocular while Paul was serious, short while Paul was tall, slight, with thin blondish wisps of hair and bright-blue eyes. They were both attractive in opposite ways.

Ordinarily she didn't respond to men's flirtations when she was committed to someone. But Paul had created a condition where it was endorsed. It was Paul, after all, who had kept trying to convince her that love and sex were two separate and unique entities. She now saw no reason to reject that philosophy.

But she had no interest in other men as sexual objects. Jesse was a romantic interest, not a sexual one. She liked him and was attracted to his looks, his sense of humor, and his intellect and thus she knew it would be dangerous to get involved with him; she might fall in love. On the other hand, having now decided to not ignore possible romantic adventures within her new point of view, she decided it would serve Paul right.

So, the office flirtation carried on as an innocent fantasy, and she had to admit, she liked it. It was fun.

And so, one Friday afternoon, Jesse asked her out for drinks after work, and she agreed but with no intention of it being more than that.

However, as such things go, after several martinis each, she rode in his Toyota Prius to his apartment, which was an old brick building close to Pioneer Square. She followed him up two flights of moldy stairs carpeted with a worn, horrid dirt red and an old banister threadbare of its finish.

The apartment was very small, a room with a small bathroom and tiny kitchen that could barely fit one person into. But she liked it. She was charmed by its minimalism. And because it was in the nucleus of town, it was likely expensive. Just off the kitchen were a small, distressed pine table and two chairs. Alongside his bed was a beat-up bookcase with books lined up haphazardly. She studied the books and saw that they were mostly nonfiction, biographies and historical.

"It isn't much, I'm afraid," Jesse said apologetically, following behind with his brief tour.

"It's very nice, Jesse," she said encouragingly.

"I'm saving up for a down payment on a condo…or something." He shrugged dubiously. "Would you like a drink?"

"Yes, please."

He poured whiskey into two short glasses and got ice out of his freezer, dropping one cube into each glass.

She sat on the sofa. He handed her glass to her and then excused himself to go to the bathroom. She stood and stared out the window at a lovely view of Elliot Bay. The air was blustery and turning purple-gray with the fading day.

When he returned from the bathroom, they sat down on the sofa. He kissed her. She held the back of his head with her left hand, encouraging him. The alcohol in her head released whatever inhibition she held previously.

They got undressed and into bed, and he entered her immediately. She gasped at this sudden penetration and didn't like it. In a matter of seconds, it seemed, he was done. She was stunned with this inconsiderate lack of foreplay. But he didn't withdraw as she expected him to. He began moving inside of her again, and she felt herself responding to his thrusts, and as he increased his pace, she began to moan, and he grimaced and grunted with each hard thrust inside of her, and as he quickened his stride on top of her not touching her except with the plunge of his desperate penis, she felt the orgasm approaching, and as she came, she screamed.

After he came a second time, he collapsed on top of her. She felt guilty about having an orgasm, almost as if it were the orgasm itself that was betraying Paul; she had succumbed to some undefined masculine power. She pondered the fact that she really liked it and was disappointed in herself that she was not in control of the situation.

While still inside of her, he began to move again.

"What! Again?"

He didn't answer but continued to thrust inside of her. As the minutes passed, she found herself exclaiming, "*Yes! Yes! Yes!*" as if giving constant approval of the act.

They lay entwined, catching their breath, sated and drained.

She told him she didn't want to go but had to.

She went to the bathroom to clean up, and when she came out, he was dressed and sitting on the sofa with a solemn expression. She straddled him naked her legs spread on each side of his lap, and hugged him as if they were confirmed lovers. He kissed her, and they rested their cheeks against each other. She realized that she was already falling in love with him. The flirtation had followed its logical course to intimacy and now romantic love.

She stood away from him, got dressed, and he drove her home. Not a word was spoken, as if it was understood: they had a predicament.

2.

Except at work Monday, Jesse ignored her. After an hour of this, she went up to him. "Is something wrong?"

"No."

"Then why are you ignoring me?"

"I'm not ignoring you."

"So, when are we getting together again?"

He paused uncomfortably. "I already have a girlfriend."

She stared at him ironically. "Yes, of course, I know you have a girlfriend."

"And you have a boyfriend."

"That didn't seem to bother you much when you were fucking my brains out."

His body slumped with obvious aggravation. "I don't want to complicate things."

"I see."

"You seemed to take it seriously."

"Well, if it was just a fuck you wanted, why didn't you just say so?"

He stared at her a moment. "I love my girlfriend."

She laughed and returned to her desk.

And so it was back to Paul's contention that love and sex were mutually exclusive. Her mistake had been giving Jesse the impression that she was falling in love with him. She realized that she couldn't be angry with Jesse; he was the logical one here. If they had continued to see each other, it would have had inevitable consequences to each of their "committed" relationships.

That night she made love to Paul with an atypical vigor.

———∞∞∞———

When she later told Lilyana about her experience with her colleague, Lilyana mentioned the Madonna/whore dichotomy.

"What's that?"

"It's a sociobiological theory that men have their 'Madonnas,' their wives at home taking care of the nest, while spreading their seed around the neighborhood into their 'whores.'"

"Men think like that?"

"They don't consciously think it, but it's an evolutionary theory, a way that nature propagates the species."

"Wow, I've never heard of this theory."

"But women are the same. They have been subjugated with prurient mores, but recently they are coming out of their shells with liberation."

"What do you mean?"

"While men have their Madonnas and whores, women marry the accountant or whoever to support the home and then fuck the cable guy or whoever while the hubby's at work."

Roslyn laughed.

"See, the mistake you made is that you took your encounter with your colleague too seriously. He might change his tune if you were to tell him that you just want to see him once in a while to just fuck each other brains out. He was a good lover, you said."

She laughed. "He was indefatigable!"

"Well, then!"

"But I guess I'm just not like that."

"You think you're not like that, due to generations of social mores, established by men, by the way... The theory goes on to suggest that men are attracted to women with large breasts and wide hips because they subconsciously are attracted to these women in evolutionary terms, as mothers who will bear strong children. And women are attracted to good-looking, powerful men for the same reason: it strengthens the species over time."

"Didn't Hitler have a similar idea?"

"You're right! Those fucking fascist sociobiologists!"

They laughed.

3.

Paul and Roslyn drove up to visit Paul's aunt and uncle on their farm on Camano Island, about sixty miles north of Seattle, where they had eighty acres. They grew their own food and had cattle, horses, goats, chickens, one golden retriever, and two Australian shepherds.

"Uncle Dave is of an independent mindset," Paul told her as they passed miles of flat farmland on each side of I-5 with "Trump in 2020" signs sprouting on each side of I-5 like weeds. The early morning sun was brilliant against sparse purple-gray clouds.

"Lots of Trump supporters around these them parts." Roslyn said.

Paul shook his head and grumbled. "Yes, Republicans everywhere. Uncle Dave, however, is more of a libertarian, believes each of us should be responsible for ourselves without depending on handouts from anyone else, especially from the government. He's totally disengaged from politics. I disagree with him, of course, on some issues, but I respect him immensely."

"Is he your father's brother?"

"Yes."

"You don't talk about your father."

"No."

"Why not?"

"My father is a bit of a fuck-up."

She stared at him. "Could you elaborate on that somewhat?"

"He's an alcoholic. I haven't heard from him in years and have no interest in doing so. Uncle Dave stays in contact."

He didn't seem to want to carry on with the subject, so she let it go.

"As far as Uncle Dave, as a kid I spent most of my summers there helping him, bailing hay, tending the horses, mending fences. I loved it. Everything I know about working with my hands I learned from Uncle Dave. He taught me how to milk a cow, ride a horse, build a barn, even rebuild an engine."

On the island they drove up a long, winding driveway, which led to a large two-story home with cedar shakes. Behind the home was a large barn. Fenced behind the barn were horses.

When Paul knocked on the door, he was met with vicious sounding barks from a dog. When the door opened, however, a golden retriever ran out to them whining and wagging his tail. Inside the cabin, Roslyn was introduced to a tall, lean man of about sixty, his face dirt brown and crosshatched from years of sun exposure. He stooped over almost painfully from what was obviously a bad back as he hugged Paul and put a huge calloused right hand gently around Roslyn's hand after being introduced.

The dog kept running around Paul and Roslyn, seeking attention. Paul tried to pet him, but he wouldn't sit still.

"Jack! Go lay down!"

The dog immediately slithered away and lay down with a thud, smiling at Paul and panting.

A short, robust woman hugged Paul and then Roslyn as if they were old friends. This was Aunt Hannah.

"Coffee?" she said.

"Sounds great, Aunt Hannah," Paul said.

Aunt Hannah disappeared into the kitchen while Uncle Dave tossed a piece of firewood into the wood-burning stove.

"How was the ride?" Dave said, as they all sat down.

"Very peaceful," Paul said.

"I hate driving into Seattle these days, with the traffic and congestion."

"I know—it's absurd."

"And all the homeless!" Aunt Hannah added.

"That too is absurd, has been for quite some time."

Aunt Hannah brought out a tray with a coffee pot and four cups. Dave poured the coffee while Hannah returned to the kitchen and returned with two slices of blackberry pie, handing each to Paul and Roslyn.

The coffee and pie were the most delicious things she had ever tasted and said so.

"Thank you," Hannah said and chuckled wryly at the compliment.

After their repast, Uncle Dave took them outside to see the horses, Jack prancing along excitedly. Paul seemed impressed how Roslyn leaped up into the saddle of a horse as Uncle Dave took them on a tour of the property, thick with Douglas fir and western red cedar, Jack dancing along. Two Australian shepherds joined them.

Back inside, Dave fed the stove another piece of firewood. Hannah fixed soup and turkey-Havarti cheese sandwiches with homemade bread.

Roslyn couldn't believe how delicious it all was. Was it the food or the ambience? Or the two combined?

When they left, they all hugged again, and Dave said to Paul, "My offer still stands."

Paul nodded. "I know. I'm still thinking about it."

In the car winding their way back out onto the street, Roslyn said, "What did your uncle mean by 'My offer still stands'?"

"He's offered me a piece of his property to build a house."

"What? For how much?"

"For free. He's even offered to help me build it. He loves building houses, from the foundation up."

"Are you kidding me?"

Paul shrugged. "No. But of course it isn't practical. We'd have to quit our jobs."

She stared at him. "We?"

Paul glanced at her. "I wouldn't do it without you."

She laughed. "It's ridiculous. Are you really thinking about it?"

"I fantasize about it all the time, especially when I'm struck in Seattle traffic."

"No shit... I envy your aunt and uncle."

"Don't. He won't be able to keep it up forever. He thinks he will, but he won't."

"Maybe that's why he wants you there."

Paul nodded. "He built and gave houses to each of his daughters, and they are married to deadbeat husbands who can't keep a job. They don't do shit there except drink shitty beer and watch Fox News. Any maintenance that needs doing on the houses is done by Dave."

"You're the son he never had."

Paul didn't disagree. "It's not as romantic as it seems. It's hard work, from sunup to sunset."

Roslyn stared out at the passing scenery dreamily.

"And I love Seattle," Paul said. "But yeah, the absurd development and the traffic's getting to me."

"I wouldn't mind breathing fresh air, growing my own food, riding horses."

"By the way, I didn't know you knew how to ride a horse."

"Why? Is there something to it?"

"What do you mean?"

"I've never been on a horse before in my life."

4.

When a particular woman caught Paul's attention, he invariably would fanaticize what this woman looked like naked, creating an approximation of the idea compared to the reality. Oftentimes this would become an obsession, especially if he encountered this woman on a regular basis. This obsession thus was based not so much on the physical but the emotional. Paul pursued a subjective ideal in women and was therefore never disappointed in the reality. He did not necessarily pursue conventional beauty, since he saw a level of beauty in just about all women. He was not interested in women with breast implants, for example, since that conveyed a false image of perfection that was to him disfigurement.

One of these obsessions became a woman who came to work in the office. She had the initial appearance of what many superficial men might refer to as "ugly." She had a strikingly large head and a mane of wild brunette hair like a male lion. She was about six feet tall and soft looking, no doubt outweighing him by twenty pounds or more. He envisioned this woman naked with expansive flesh, plump with hospitable fat. The reality became humungous breasts that sagged once removed from the constraints of a bra and the law of gravity. He buried his head into these glands, smothering himself with moans. They made love an extraordinarily long time, he exploring each inch of her colossal body, his hands moving softly over her smooth skin so white it looked as if it had never seen the sun. He observed her orgasm from the observation of her portly pubis, face flushed red as she screamed out almost painfully, her teeth clenched and teeming with saliva as if caught in a seizure or an electrical shock. It went on for a full minute.

When he went into her bathroom to pee, she followed him in.

"What are you doing!" he said, laughing.

"I want to watch you pee."

He sat down on the toilet.

"You sit when you pee?"

"It's become a habit since my girlfriend insists on it."

"Oh. You have a girlfriend."

"Yes. Don't you have a boyfriend?"

"No... Do you love her?"

"Very much."

"I don't understand."

"What don't you understand?"

"Why you live with someone who you say you love very much and make love to me."

He had no response, since he had no answer. He dabbed the end of his penis with a square of toilet paper and stood.

"Nevertheless," she said, "I would like to keep seeing you. I liked fucking you."

"All right," he said vaguely, flushing then washing his hands.

However, once this subjective quest for the disclosure of a woman's complete physical body had been realized, he as a rule had no desire to carry this relationship further. And since they worked together, he knew that continuing with an office romance was dangerous since it might become complicated by love—or hate—neither sentiment an auspicious one for working together.

And since Kathy knew about Roslyn, it rather surprised him that she wanted to keep seeing him. He had expected her to be, if anything, angry. He certainly didn't love her and knew her well enough to know that it was unlikely he ever would. He decided if he did continue to see her, it would continue on his terms only, and if she objected, that would be fine too.

It was Roslyn who held the hallowed spot in his life, and no other woman would ever interfere with that. His pursuit of other women was an external part of his life separate from the complete being, Roslyn. She was an integral part of him and to lose her would be tantamount to losing a leg, his vision, or some other animate part of him.

5.

Paul read an article online that included an interview with a climate scientist in which he said that the expectation of inevitable global catastrophe due to climate change was unavoidable because the propaganda against doing anything about it by the deniers was too powerful. It also had proceeded to a near "tipping point," in that even if the world stopped putting CO_2 into the atmosphere right now, it was probably too late.

This was creating what he saw in his colleagues symptoms of "pre-traumatic-stress syndrome," which was also occurring among much of the population, with behavior such as "anger, denial, panic, binge drinking; and obsessive, intrusive thoughts similar to what soldiers experience after coming home from a war environment."

In this article, it said renowned biologist Paul Ehrlich had written a paper saying that the sixth extinction was already happening, with thousands of species going extinct daily, and he put civilization's chances of survival at 10 percent, and even that he considered optimistic. Asked what he did to cope with this, he quipped: "I drink a lot."

Paul had noticed this exact phenomenon in his friends and acquaintances, who for the most part avoided talking or even thinking about climate change, preferring instead to party.

But didn't his generation have an obligation to face this potential catastrophe head-on and attempt to do something about it? On the other hand, what was the point, if as the climate scientist said, the tipping point had passed? Wasn't partying the most logical response? He in fact was little different than his friends: he too escaped into alcohol, marijuana, and sex. He continued to ponder Uncle Dave's offer.

This political, economic, and ecological stage they inhabited seemed also to be having a negative effect on his relationship with Roslyn. One evening they were driving to a party at some friends' home in Ballard. On the way, the mood between them was somber; hardly a word between them was spoken. When he looked over at her, she was staring at the road ahead with a lost look. What had he done now? He suddenly became furious.

At the party they separated to mingle with the others, and when they drove home, again nothing passed their lips in the way of conversation. They went straight to bed without a word. Paul was so angry he couldn't sleep. He rose to fix himself a nightcap, staring out the front window at the lights of the Wallingford District.

When he returned to bed, Roslyn grabbed him tight and said: "Where did you go!"

"I couldn't sleep, so I went out and fixed myself a drink."

"I thought you had left me!"

"I'm right here."

He realized that she was dreaming and felt better about everything.

In the morning, however, the accursed muteness resumed. They were having coffee. Finally, he said, "Roslyn, what's wrong?"

"Nothing."

"Don't say nothing. I know something is wrong. You have to talk to me."

"It's the same old issue."

He of course knew what that issue was and so didn't pursue it.

She said: "I just want us to quit our jobs and get away from it all."

"All what?"

"All this. Your fucking whores. This fucking city and its fucking bullshit."

"Take Uncle Dave up on his offer?"

"Why not?"

"Because, honey, we're dug in. We have jobs. We're stuck here like everyone else, fighting the traffic. We can't just quit our jobs and run off to some nonexistent paradise."

"We'll sell the house, build a home on the island. I can waitress again, if I have to. You can get drive a school bus or something."

"Interesting you mentioned that."

"Why?"

"Because I've been thinking the same thing. It's just that…"

"What?"

"The grass is not always greener just has more cowshit."

"All I know is that I can't continue on like this. I thought I could get used to it, but I can't."

It didn't seem to occur to Roslyn that there were women on Camano Island too.

That night he had a dream that he was making love to an enormous black woman, a woman with cumulous waves of fat. They were in front of the bathroom mirror. Her body was bent over holding onto the sink, his legs spread against her huge behind, her enormous breasts swinging this way and that out of sync. He was frustrated because he wanted to come but couldn't.

He awoke, realizing it was a dream. He was lying on his back with a throbbing erection, Roslyn next to him breathing heavily. He got up to go to the bathroom and relieve himself over the sink, thinking about the enormous black woman.

Back in bed, he wondered if he would really make love to a woman that big. He realized with revelation that he indeed would and, furthermore, had.

Would it be possible for them to move onto the island where his chances of erotic engagements would be reduced? It occurred to him that this was the major reason for his reluctance to make the move, not to mention the distance away from Lilyana.

6.

When Paul told Lilyana he was thinking of selling everything and moving onto his uncle's property on Camano Island, she had no reply.

"Well—what do you think?"

"You're not serious, is what I think."

"But I am. I'm seriously thinking about it."

"And Roslyn?"

"She's on board with the idea, maybe more than I am."

"How would you live?"

"I'll have money from my house. My uncle is giving me a lot and is going to help me build a house. If we have to, we'll get jobs."

"Doing what?"

"Anything. We wouldn't need much. A bartender, whatever."

She laughed. "Do you know anything about living that kind of life?"

"A little. Enough to understand what I'm getting into."

They were sitting up in Lilyana's bed sipping wine after making love.

"Aren't you going to ask if we'll ever see each other?"

"I would assume not."

"It's not that far away. I'll be down to Seattle on occasion to see you."

Lilyana sipped her wine reflectively. "But not as much as we are now."

"No, probably not."

She nodded. "When you come, I want you to bring Roslyn."

He looked at her. "You and Roslyn have become good friends, haven't you?"

She nodded, without elaborating. "Oh, well, all good things come to an end."

As Paul was leaving, she said: "I have something for you."

"Okay."

She went to get the nude painting of Roslyn.

He stared at it as if not believing what he was seeing. He held it at arm's length and scrutinized it. "When did you do this?"

"I finished it recently."

"Did Roslyn pose nude for you? Oh, never mind, of course she did. You've captured her beautifully."

"Thank you."

He kissed her goodbye and carried the painting away under his right arm.

When he left, she poured more wine and picked up her brush, staring at a nearly finished painting. She hadn't heard from Peter in some time, and she wondered if her life was abandoning her. She wasn't getting any younger.

A few days later as she was shopping at the Pike Place Market, a man approached her and said, "Aren't you Lilyana?"

She looked back at this man and didn't recognize him. He was a middle-aged man with a close-cropped gray beard and round, rimless glasses and intense blue eyes.

"Yes, I'm sorry, I don't remember you."

"I met you at a party where you were with Peter Placik."

"Ah."

"I'm terribly sorry about Peter."

"What?"

"Peter...oh my god, you didn't know?"

"Know what?"

"Well...he committed suicide. I hate being the one to tell you."

She dropped her canvas shopping bag in the busy street and felt her knees buckle. He held her up.

"I'm so sorry! I had assumed you knew." He carefully let her go.

"When?"

"A few weeks ago. He had found out that he was in the fourth stage of throat cancer. He apparently didn't want to go through the treatment."

7.

The American monarch butterfly is considered the most beautiful of all butterflies, and thus its name, monarch.

Monarch butterflies go through four stages during their life and through four generations a year.

In February and March, the final generation of hibernating monarch butterflies comes out, each searching for a mate. They then migrate north and east in order to find a place to lay their eggs. This is stage one and generation one of the new year.

In March and April, the eggs are laid on milkweed plants. They hatch into larvae. In about two weeks, the caterpillar is full-grown and finds a place to attach itself to start the process of metamorphosis, transforming into chrysalis. The following ten days is a time of rapid metamorphosis, transforming into what makes the beautiful butterfly what it is. It will emerge from the pulpa and fly away feeding on flowers and pollinating in the short time that it has. This first generation will lay eggs for the following generation.

The second generation is born in May and June, the third in July and August.

The fourth generation is different from the first three. It is born in September and October and goes through the same process as the first three. However, the fourth generation of monarch butterfly migrates to warmer climates in California and Mexico, living six to eight months until it is time to begin the whole process again.

Monarch butterflies are the only insect that migrates to warmer climates up to 2,500 miles away. But the number of migrating butterflies has diminished precipitately due to agriculture and climate change. The milkweed plants on which monarch butterflies lay their eggs have mostly been cleared for agribusiness growing corn and soy. To farmers, milkweed is considered a weed that interferes with their crops and is removed with herbicides. But to the monarch butterfly, milkweed is a necessary component of the ecosystem for survival. Because of this, GMOs, and a warming climate, scientists now believe that the monarch butterfly population has diminished 90 percent.

Monarch butterflies have been with us at least 50 million years. Besides their obvious aesthetic value, these billions of butterflies and moths indicate a healthy ecosystem. Like bees, they are an essential part of life because they pollinate and act as a natural pest control. They are an essential element in the food chain and are prey for birds, bats, and other insectivorous animals. The fluttering of the monarch butterfly's wings is essential for the diversity of life.

On this plot of land that was given to Paul, he and Roslyn lived in a yurt while their house was being built. He and Uncle Dave had already laid the cement foundation and had erected the basic structure. They still had to put on the roof, the cedar siding, install the flooring, the plumbing, electricity, and sheetrock.

Paul was happier than he had ever been.

He and Roslyn had planted on their property an orchard of apple, pear, and plum trees. In the spring they had cultivated a vegetable garden. Paul and Roslyn tended to the animals and helped Uncle Paul on the property with a multitude of chores. They milked the cows, gathered the eggs from the chickens, and sold the raw milk and eggs at the farmers' market in Stanwood.

Every day they went horseback riding.

There was a ridge on the property that offered a spectacular view of Puget Sound. One warm September evening they were on the ridge, prepared to view the setting sun.

"Are you happy?" Roslyn said.

"Very. Are you?"

"Yes." She nodded and tilted her head against his shoulder. "Happier than I've ever been."

Suddenly, a flock of monarch butterflies appeared in front of them, fluttering erratically from bush to bush, from flower to flower, from one grass blade to another.

"They're beautiful!" Roslyn said, reaching up into the air and managing to capture one between her cupped hands.

"What are you going to do with it?" Paul said.

She raised her arms into the air, spread them out like wings, and watched the butterfly flitter off this way and that and then blend with the others catching the southern wind.

The End

CPSIA information can be obtained
at www.ICGtesting.com
Printed in the USA
LVHW031139080221
678694LV00001B/27